CRIME, UP CLOSE AND PERSONAL

STORIES OF MYSTERY AND SUSPENSE

DAVID H. HENDRICKSON

"I can't believe you just called," Nate said in a somber tone that made Jimmy think someone had died.

"What's wrong? The storm hasn't even hit landfall yet."

"Jimmy, this is spooky."

"Spooky? How?"

"There's a mission, but... it's hopeless. A suicide mission." Nate sighed. "The mayor suggested I send you, but I refused. I'm not going to sacrifice you. I just got off the phone with him. But then you called."

"What's the mission?"

"I can't."

"What's the damned mission?"

PRAISE FOR DAVID H. HENDRICKSON

"A fantastic writer, one of our best working right now." - Dean Wesley Smith, *USA Today* bestselling writer

"David H. Hendrickson is one of my favorite writers."- Kristine Kathryn Rusch, *USA Today* bestselling writer

Crime, Up Close and Personal
Stories of Mystery and Suspense

Published by Pentucket Publishing
www.pentucketpublishing.com
Cover illustration by skyfotostock1/depositphotos.com
Cover design by Annie Reed

"Buried Braces" originally appeared in *Mystery, Crime, and Mayhem: Cold Cases*, edited by Leah Cutter, Knotted Row Press, November, 2022

"Santa's Shrinkage," originally appeared in the *WMG Holiday Spectacular 2021*, edited by Kristine Kathryn Rusch, WMG Publishing, Inc., December, 2021

"Chimichangas and a Couple of Glocks," originally appeared in *Guns & Tacos, Volume 5*, edited by Michael Bracken and Trey R. Barker, Down & Out Books, September, 2021

"Too Many Idiots, Too Few Boats," originally appeared in *Thrill Ride – the Magazine: Betrayal*, edited by M.L. Buchman, Buchman Bookworks, Inc., December, 2023

"A Long Shot Worth Betting On," originally appeared in *Mystery, Crime, and Mayhem: Private Eyes*, edited by Leah Cutter, Knotted Row Press, July, 2020

ISBN-13: 978-1-948134-23-1

CONTENTS

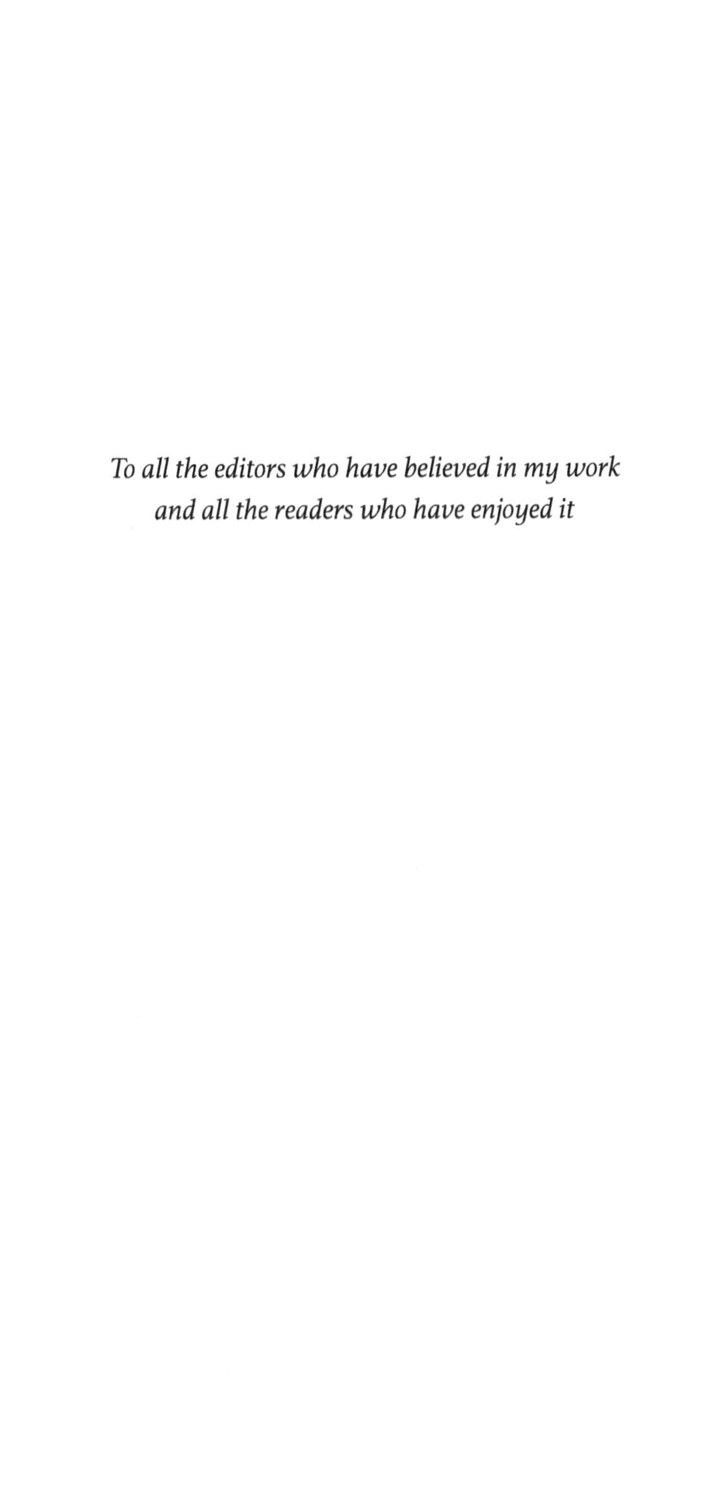

To all the editors who have believed in my work
and all the readers who have enjoyed it

INTRODUCTION

This is my tenth short story collection and my fourth in the mystery and suspense genre. The last two, both released in recent months as part of a planned rapid-fire publication schedule, included tales from different eras (*Crime from Another Time*) and those which included elements of the fantastic (*Crime Fantastique*). I arrived at those two titles early on, but one for this volume proved a bit more elusive.

For a while, I internally referred to it as my *Vanilla Crime* collection, differentiating it from the other two based on its stories being set very much in this era and not including even a hint of the paranormal. The *Vanilla Crime* title was, of course, just a placeholder, used only in internal discussions until I could figure out what to actually call it. After all, *Vanilla Crime* sounds about as boring as *The Stories that Didn't Fit* or even *The Leftovers*.

These stories are anything but boring. Or leftovers.

In fact, I briefly considered (for about a nanosecond) calling this collection *The Best of the Best* because far from being leftovers or vanilla, these stories were ones I considered to be among my very best. And if they weren't—if I couldn't accurately assess my stories' quality—at least they were among my favorites. But then what would that say about the other two collections? Were they in any way half rate? Hell, no! I considered many, if not most, of those stories to also be among my best or favorites. (Yup, I guess I love them all.)

What I finally realized was that what binds these stories together isn't just what they aren't (from another era or paranormal) or what they might or might not be in terms of high quality or most-favored status. What binds them together is how up close and personal these tales are. In one of them, "up close" is used in a humorous sense, but in the others the tale is deadly serious. And that, all by itself, insures entry in my canon of personal favorites.

Whatever the case, I'm betting the ranch that you'll consider these stories anything but "vanilla" or "leftovers." Indeed, I'm hoping you'll soon consider them some of your own personal favorites.

BURIED BRACES

INTRODUCTION TO BURIED BRACES

I wrote this story for *Mystery, Crime, and Mayhem: Cold Cases*. I began with only a general idea of where I was going, as is often the case, but the further I got, the more I took on my detective's obsession. The more the victim's remains haunted me. The more her short life's story pierced my heart.

Even now, years later, I remember leaning forward in my chair at times as I typed the words. It had become very much *up close and personal*.

That emotional intensity on my part apparently translated into the story's effectiveness because editor Leah Cutter nominated it for the Short Mystery Fiction Society's Derringer Award. She had only four nominations to use on all the *Mystery, Crime, and Mayhem* stories she published that year, yet she used one of them on "Buried Braces." It proved not to be a finalist, but her nomination confirmed my gut instinct that the story had hit the mark.

I won't ever forget Daniella Cefalo or those who in the real world have suffered her fate.

BURIED BRACES

Pags sipped his piping-hot, black coffee and finished off the last of the day's pointless paperwork, hunting and pecking on the computer's keyboard the same way he'd hunted and pecked on a typewriter decades ago when he was just a boot. He sat alone in the Detectives Room, nicknamed The Closet because it was no larger than a small conference room with two desks crammed U-shaped up against each of the three facing walls. Pags's retirement papers rested on the far left corner of his desk needing only his signature.

He ignored them.

It probably was time, he had to grudgingly admit. Maybe even past time. In his thirty-eight years on the force, his hair had gone from jet black to white, his torso from hard-body, washboard abs to doughboy soft, and his face from boyishly smooth to wrinkled, weathered, and gnarled.

Thirty-eight years. The last twenty-nine as Detective and then Detective-Sergeant, all here in Springvale,

Massachusetts, a one-stoplight town an hour north of Boston but in many ways, a universe removed. Springvale had more trees than asphalt and almost as many horse farms as patrol cars. His big-city cop friends in Boston and its grittier suburbs referred to Springvale as Sleepyville. They'd bust his chops asking about his top-priority case of the ghastly day in February when the Sleepyville Dunkin' Donuts ran out of Boston Kremes.

As one after another of those burned-out colleagues grabbed retirement like a drowning man clinging to life jacket, Pags could almost hear the subtext to their ball-busting banter.

Why would you ever retire? Nothing ever happens in Sleepyville! Retirement? How would you notice the difference?

As if domestic abuse cases or other assaults were only the province of the Big Bad Cities. As if the Springvale Savings Bank or Frank's Liquor Store or the Springvale Family Pharmacy had never been robbed. As if Springvale High School was immune to the opioid epidemic.

Admittedly, there had only been two murders in his thirty-eight years on the Springvale police force, and one of them really belonged to a nearby community. Compared to the body counts in the Big Bad Cities, Springvale really was Sleepyville. And both of those murders had been solved and resulted in convictions. The town's count of unsolved murders was exactly zero.

But that didn't mean Springvale's slate was clean. At least not for Pags. Twenty-five years ago, a teenage girl, Daniella Cefalo, had disappeared and had never been found. The powers that be might have written her off as a runaway who succumbed anonymously in the underworld in some Big Bad City—anywhere but squeaky-clean Springvale—but the case still haunted Pags. The first day of the month, the usual happy family photos that served as wallpaper background on his computer screen were automatically replaced by photos of Daniella.

Pags would never forget.

The damned slate was not clean. And until the slate was clean, how could he move on? Even if everyone from Lois, his wife of almost forty years, to Lee Hankinson, the new Chief of Police, thought it was time. For Lois, this was the time for them to enjoy the good life before it was too late. For Chief Hankinson—a pompous, empty suit if there ever was one—Pags's departure would mean "new blood," a euphemism for replacing a pain in the ass like Pags with a yes man who'd owe Hankinson.

Pags told himself, and mostly believed it, that he'd pull the plug if he could find Daniella Cefalo. Or far more likely, find out what had happened to her. And if there was justice to be served, get it. But he'd never quit while Daniella remained on the slate.

Springvale's slate. His slate.

They'd have to force him out.

The phone rang as Pags took another sip of his no-longer piping-hot coffee.

"Detective Pagliarulo?" came a familiar female voice on the line. Gabriella Sanchez, a junior patrol officer who'd only been on the force for a year. One of the few who called him by his formal name. "We've got something here you'll want to see."

Pags's coffee suddenly tasted bitter. He grabbed his rumpled, dark sports jacket off the back of his chair and headed for the door. In a big city, he'd be alerting his partner, but here in a Sleepyville that suddenly wasn't so sleepy, he was on his own.

THE PREVIOUS FALL, eight months ago, the Wellington Estates development had been nothing but thickly wooded acres of oak, pine, and birch trees untouched for decades. Pags thought it should have stayed that way. But the housing boom and a fortuitous location within ten minutes of I-95 and an hour from Boston while still being tucked away on a remote, newly created side street conspired to make those quiet pristine acres ripe for the picking.

And they were getting picked clean.

Pags pulled onto the newly created Wellington Avenue in his unmarked, black Chevy Impala. He drove past the first few inhabited houses and their bare hints of a lawn, the thin green blades of freshly planted grass just beginning to poke through to the surface. When the cul-de-sac split into left and right halves, he bore left and drove past a half dozen partially built houses where construction workers in yellow hard hats and on ladders pounded nails into sidings and roofs. At the end of the cul-de-sac where it curved back around on itself and the lots were still being cleared, a cruiser waited, its blue lights flashing.

Two officers, Paulie Mills and Gabriella Sanchez, stood beside a twenty-foot-high mountain of freshly excavated dirt, thirty yards to the left of a blue port-opotty. They were talking to four bulky men—three darkly tanned white men and an African American—dressed in sweat-stained wife beaters, grimy jeans, dirt-coated work boots, and hard hats. One of them, the oldest of the white men with gray hair and heavily tattooed arms, was gesturing angrily. Presumably the foreman.

At this far end of the development, felled trees had been hauled away but yellow heavy equipment—a backhoe loader, power shovel, bulldozer, and dump truck—had been in the process of digging up tree roots to make way for smooth lawns and deep cellars.

Had been in the digging process. Pags didn't need decades of detective experience to guess that the men had been working on the heavy equipment when something stopped them. And the foreman was none too happy about it.

"What's up?" Pags asked Mills, the senior officer. Pushing fifty and balding with a bulbous nose covered with a spiderweb of prominent red blood vessels, Mills was a lazy SOB, coasting into the same retirement that Pags dreaded. They'd locked horns time after time over the years.

"These two officers are telling us we can't dig!" the foreman began, stepping closer, wiping sweat and caked dirt off his brow. He smelled of a hard day's work. The other three members of his crew stood behind him, nodding.

Pags held up his hand in a stopping gesture. He pointed to the two officers. "I want to hear it from these two."

Gabriella Sanchez, the junior officer who had summoned Pags, pointed to Mills in deference.

"We've got a crime scene here," Mills said. "These guys were digging a cellar with that power shovel over there and scooped up the remains of a body. Actually, not much when it comes to remains. Just a skeleton. Busted it up pretty good."

"We didn't know nothing was there!" the foreman protested. "How was we to know? Joey called it right in, not really thinking. He had no idea you guys would shut us down."

"So if he'd known we'd shut you down, you'd have kept your mouth shut and kept on digging?" Pags asked.

"I dunno," the foreman said, crossing his thick arms. "This never happened before."

"You sure?" Pags asked, eyeing both the foreman and the rest of the crew. "Any other skeletons here or at any other site that I should know about? Times you just kept digging?"

"No!" they replied in near unison.

Pags detected no unease from any of them, only surprise. "Okay, then, but right now, this is a crime scene. I'll need to see what you dug up."

"When can we get back to digging?" the foreman asked. "We got a tight schedule here."

Pags fixed the foreman with an icy glare. "Explain that to the corpse."

With the late afternoon May sun and Daylight Savings Time, Pags figured he'd have about another three hours of sun.

He used all of it.

The power shovel had ripped the skeleton into three mangled pieces: the upper body, the midsection, and the lower body consisting of the hips and legs. The damage had been unintentional, of course. The work crew had never suspected a body had been buried there decades earlier, and work had stopped as soon as the men spotted bones poking out of the shovelful of dirt scooped out of the ground and deposited off to the side on the twenty-foot-high mound of earth.

But the violation hit Pags hard nonetheless. All deaths were heart-rending to some degree, and a secretly buried body pointed strongly to the far end of that spectrum. There could be no happy end to this story. But to have its epilogue be a crushing rending of the skeletal remains seemed an unconscionable indignity.

Taking photos with his phone during every step of the way, Pags exposed partially submerged bones, pawed carefully at the soil to uncover additional fragments of the skeleton, then packaged them all with the surrounding soil in evidence bags. The odds were slim to none that some stray piece of evidence, a hair or clothing fiber or some other random element, existed in that soil and contained DNA that linked this body to what had happened, but Pags had to try.

There were no tattered remnants of clothing, not yet fully decomposed. No rings or earrings.

Nothing but bones.

The sun moved lower on the horizon. A sharp pain stabbed him in the back of his eyes. He was running out of time.

Pags's blood ran cold when he uncovered an intact skull, but he kept going, methodically and patiently, until eventually, in his mind, he could array the grisly collection into its original form, from skull to toes. Big cities had dedicated forensic teams to help detectives with the analysis. In Springvale, Pags was on his own. He was no forensic specialist and the lab just outside of Boston would weigh in with the official results. But to his imperfect eye, the identity of the reconstructed skeleton was unmistakable.

Daniella Cefalo.

Fifteen years old when she went missing twenty-five years ago. Barely five feet tall and petite, Daniella had been pretty, with long, auburn-colored hair and sparkling green eyes. Athletic. Played on the Springvale High girls' soccer and softball teams. Popular. With a bubbling, outgoing personality, according to the file, every line long since memorized by Pags.

None of that was visible now. She'd stopped being bubbling and outgoing, athletic and popular, twenty-five years ago.

There was nothing pretty about that skeleton. Even before the power shovel had crushed so many of the bones, tearing them apart. She was no longer discernably auburn-haired, or any kind of hair at all. Her green eyes, long since decayed to nothing, no longer sparkled.

But Pags had no doubts it was Daniella. Her smiling

face had beamed out at him on his various computers for twenty-five years.

A smiling face with bright white teeth covered by orthodontic braces.

Braces now corroded and dangling from the skeleton's teeth.

BACK AT HIS desk in the Detectives Room, once again alone, Pags pulled the file out of the locked bottom right drawer of his desk. He had the whole damned thing all but memorized, of course. But he wanted to see the facts fresh yet again with his own eyes. And though a copy of every last page had been uploaded to the server, and he'd downloaded a local copy to his laptop, a dinosaur like him always preferred the paper copy.

Lois wouldn't be waiting for him. He'd told her hours ago not to wait up. He wasn't twenty-nine or thirty-nine or even fifty-nine anymore. But right now, he was ready to stay up all night and keep going the next day.

Dinosaurs got fueled by outrage, too. And Pags's fire burned hot.

He accessed the Department of Motor Vehicles database and got updated addresses for the most significant names in the file, most notably for Johnny Dupree, Daniella Cefalo's boyfriend at the time of her disappearance. Dupree had had an apparently air-tight alibi, passed a polygraph test, and been overcome with grief—overcome was actually far too weak a word, he'd been slaughtered by it—but it was the logical first step to retrace.

Really the only step to retrace. Daniella Cefalo had been the only child to a single mom, a mother so destroyed by her daughter's death that she took her own life less than a year later. With no siblings, the father unknown, and estranged aunts, uncles, and cousins in distant states, there wasn't a single living blood relative to Daniella.

Twenty-five years ago, Pags had spoken to every other member of the freshman class, all thirty-eight of them, as well as Daniella's teammates and coaches on the softball and soccer teams. Then he'd added any other possible students she'd interacted with. They all spoke as if in unison. Everyone loved Daniella. No one had a single bad thing to say about her. And they couldn't imagine her running away.

So it was Johnny Dupree or bust.

Dupree now lived south of Boston in Quincy. Pags would be lucky to get there by ten, and that was assuming there was no Celtics, Bruins, or Red Sox game letting out, tangling the Southeast Expressway into an eleven o'clock arrival.

The easy way out was to call Johnny Dupree and feel him out by phone. But Pags wanted to see Dupree's face, wondered if it would betray a hidden secret when confronted by a ghost from his past.

Pags wasn't taking the easy way out. Danielle Cefalo deserved better. Her fate had been anything but the easy way out.

DUPREE'S HOUSE, a dark brown split-level with a wide, wooden front porch, was shrouded in darkness, illuminated only by the meager light cast by a streetlamp thirty yards down the quiet side street and the blueish glow coming from a TV deep within. Hanging potted flowers dotted the porch ceiling every ten feet.

Pags took the front steps two at a time and rang the bell. It chimed loudly, but for long seconds nothing happened. Finally, the overhead porch light beamed on.

Dupree answered the door wearing slippers and striped pajamas beneath a navy-blue bathrobe. Pags recognized him right away from the file despite the passage of twenty-five years, years that had not been kind to the boyish fifteen-year-old in Pags's memory and the original photographs. Dupree was now average height with a pronounced beer belly, albeit well cloaked by the bathrobe. He wore dark-rimmed glasses, and his thinning black hair was askew. He looked very annoyed.

"What do you want?" Dupree demanded, showing no recognition of Pags. "Do you realize what time it is?"

Pags knew exactly what time it was. It was 10:43 pm. He'd run into Sox post-game traffic right after he crossed the Tobin Bridge into Boston. It was rude to be calling on someone so late, but Pags didn't really care.

"Johnny Dupree?" Pags asked.

"Yeah, John Dupree. No one's called me Johnny in a long time." He squinted. "Do I know you?"

Pags flashed his badge. "I'm Detective Pagliarulo.

With the Springvale police force. Springvale, where you grew up until your family moved to Boxford."

"Yeah, I know where I grew up," Dupree said testily. He smelled of beer and stale sweat. "What do you want?"

"May I come in?"

"Depends on what you want. I haven't been in Springvale in years."

"There've been some developments in an old case. I just need to ask a few questions. See if we missed anything. Strictly routine." Pags waited while Dupree stared blankly. "I need just a few minutes of your time."

A female voice called from another room far inside the house. "Who is it?"

"It's awfully late," Dupree said to Pags. "Could you come back tomorrow?"

"No. I need to talk to you now," Pags said. "I drove all the way down here from Springvale. Hit all the Sox post-game traffic. That's why I'm so late. I apologize, but I need to talk to you now."

Dupree stepped aside and was about to usher Pags in when dawning realization crossed his face. "I know you. You're that detective from..." Dupree's face hardened. "You gave me a really hard time back then. Is that what this is about? Is that the old case? This is about Daniella?"

"Yes," Pags said. "May I come in?"

"No," Dupree said. "I'm not talking about her in front of my wife."

Dupree called over his shoulder. "It's just an old... an old guy from the neighborhood where I grew up. Go ahead without me. We'll be a few minutes."

Dupree stepped out onto the porch. He led them into the shadows, thirty feet from the light above the front door, next to a wooden railing. He lit a cigarette and drew in deeply. He leaned back against the dark wood paneling of the front wall, then turned his head to avoid blowing smoke in Pags's face.

"Is she... is Daniella...?" Dupree winced, then looked away. He knew the answer to the unfinished question. It was written all over his pained face. But he didn't want to say the words.

Pags eyed Dupree for long seconds. Dupree took another drag from the cigarette. Its embers glowed.

"We'll need official confirmation from the lab," Pags finally said, "but we're quite sure we've found Daniella's remains."

Dupree's shoulders slumped. He looked like he'd been slugged in the gut.

"Where?" he asked.

"We aren't making that information public quite yet. That's one reason why I needed to speak to you tonight."

"You don't need me to..." Dupree's face turned a sickly greenish pallor. "Need me to identify—"

"No," Pags said. He spared Dupree the obvious fact that after decades there was nothing left to identify. No pretty face, green eyes, and autumn-colored hair.

Just bones and teeth. Bones, teeth, and braces.

"Oh, God," Dupree said, apparently filling in the blanks himself. "She's... she really is dead. Gone for good." He drew hard on the cigarette. "I mean, I knew she couldn't possibly still be alive after all these years. But you still hold out hope, you know? Even after you move on. You have to move on. You can't wait forever, especially when you know deep inside she ain't never coming back. She's gone. Gone for good." He glanced toward the front door. "Daniella was my first love. So sweet. So pretty. I was wild about her. Everyone loved her. She didn't have an enemy in the world."

Pags waited for Dupree to continue, but he just shook his head.

"Can I get you a beer?" Dupree asked. He licked his lips. "I sure could use a cold one myself."

Pags shook his head no. He didn't want one and he didn't want Dupree having another, either. "Tell me again about the last time you saw Daniella."

"Am I a suspect? *Again*?" Dupree asked, incredulous. He pushed himself off the wall and got in Pags's face. "After all these years? You still think I could have killed her? Is that why you're here?"

Pags took a half step backward and held out his hands in a back-off gesture.

"I don't know who killed her," he said. "That's what I'm trying to find out."

"I *loved* her!" Dupree said, stabbing Pags in the chest with his index finger. "I know you think now, just like you thought back then, that we were just fifteen so it couldn't have really meant anything. We were just stupid kids." He glanced toward the front door, leaned close, and lowered his voice. "She was the love of my life. The one. The only. I fell in and out of love after that, sure. That's how life goes. But nothing ever measured up to what I felt for Daniella. I never could have hurt her. I loved her like I never, ever loved again."

Pags waited, hoping Dupree would keep talking, but the man fell silent and fell back against the wall, a distant look in his eyes.

"So what happened on that last day you saw her?" Pags finally asked.

Dupree stared at Pags, took a hard drag on the cigarette, then blew the smoke in Pags's face.

Pags waited. Dupree finally nodded.

"It was a long time ago, but I remember it like it was yesterday," he said. "It was near the end of our freshman year and we were looking forward to all the things we could do that summer. Neither of us could drive, of course. We were just fifteen. So we needed one of our parents to drive us everywhere. But we could still bike down to the pond or over to the other one's house and just hang out. Listen to music and stuff. Or just talk. We'd been doing a lot of that, mostly at my house 'cause it was bigger and had A/C and I had more CDs.

"She couldn't come over after school that day. That had been happening a lot lately. Said she had too much studying to do. She'd been studying pretty hard but been having trouble concentrating for some reason.

"She'd been arguing with her mom a lot. I guess her mom thought we were going too fast. Said we were just kids. We hadn't gone all the way, you know? I wanted to, God knows, and for a while there we'd been coming close. We'd been going out for eight months, so it felt like forever.

"But her mom said we were only kids and we needed to slow the hell down. Said I was just going to use Daniella and then dump her like some guy did to her, to

Daniella's mom, sixteen years before. Got her pregnant and then disappeared. Daniella never knew her father. Never met him. Never even knew who he was. And her mom compared me to that dirtbag. Can you believe that?"

Dupree shook his head, disgusted.

"I guess Daniella listened because we slowed way the hell down," he said. "Hardly did anything anymore. I was wondering if she was even interested in me anymore, but she said that wasn't true. We just had to slow down for a while. That's all it was.

"No way I ever would have hurt her. I loved her, man. And no way she ever would have run away like you guys tried to say. That wasn't her at all."

Pags had never agreed with that official conclusion put out by the powers that be but wasn't about to stop Dupree and make that correction. Pags wanted the verbal locomotive to keep rolling down the tracks.

And it did.

"And if she had run away," Dupree continued, "she'd have never run away alone. Not without me. Not without at least talking to me about it. Hell, if it had come down to it, I'd have gone with her." He shook his head. "She didn't run away. She just disappeared. As soon as she got home that day, she called her mother at work to check in, gave me a quick call and said she'd be studying, and then... nothing.

"When her mom got home from work later that night, the house was empty. She thought she must have misunderstood her phone conversation with Daniella. *Hoped* she'd misunderstood the conversation. *Prayed* she'd misunderstood it and Daniella was really over at my house.

"But she wasn't. Her mom called us and talked to my mom. But Daniella wasn't there. She was gone. For good."

Pags watched Dupree replaying the events of that night in his vacant eyes. No one was that good of an actor.

IF IT WAS rude for Pags to call on Johnny Dupree—now John Dupree—at 10:40 pm, it was supremely obnoxious to ring his parents' doorbell after midnight. What's worse, the home and its connected three-car garage on this secluded side street reeked of money: a massive Colonial on a two-acre, tree-lined lot with a stone walkway that bisected a thick, immaculately manicured lawn. The smell of chlorine in the air betrayed the existence of a large swimming pool in the backyard, and a tennis court was barely visible from the edge of the circular driveway.

Not the sort of resident who would be amused by a visit after midnight, if such an animal even existed. However, also not a Springvale resident. Not a taxpayer who paid Pag's salary. This was a resident of Boxford, where the entire population was quite convinced that their turds did not stink.

So to hell with them.

After twenty-five years of nothing, Pags had to strike while the iron was hot. He'd warned everyone from Officers Mills and Sanchez to the members of the work crew to even Johnny Dupree himself—John Dupree—to keep their mouths shut and tell no one—no one!—about the uncovered body or in the case of Dupree, Pags's revisiting of the same questions he'd asked twenty-five years ago.

Word would inevitably leak out sooner or later, but Springvale really was Sleepyville in terms of press coverage. The *Boston Globe* didn't care, and Springvale's own regional rag didn't cover much more than the town Selectmen's and School Committee meetings and PTA bake sales. Its writers couldn't even spell investigative journalism. And praise be for that!

Pags always wanted to see reactions first-hand when he broke news. After word got out, calm features could be composed and careful responses rehearsed.

In this case, here at the house of the senior Duprees, Eileen and Randall, Pags hoped the mother would answer the door. The father had been a hotshot executive back then, too busy with his business wheeling and dealing to be much involved in his son's life. The mother was the key to her son's alibi that he'd come straight home from school, gone to his room, and played video games until the fateful call from Daniella Cefalo's mother. The phone records and forensics on the video game's internal computer had corroborated the alibi, but Pags didn't have much else to go on.

Daniella's mother had committed suicide. The father Daniella had never known, and who paid no alimony, lived in Los Angeles and was confirmed to have been there the entire week leading up to the disappearance. In all of Springvale High, there had been no known enemies or rivals. No boys who lined up as spurned lovers.

Other than some random serial killer who'd happened to stumble on Springvale, Johnny Dupree was the only possible link. And with his alibi apparently airtight, Pags was left with only one string left to pull: Eileen Dupree's corroboration that her son had gone up to his room and remained there until the fateful, panicked call from Daniella's mother.

Eileen Dupree wouldn't be the first devoted mother to cover up for her son's crimes.

Pags wanted to look her in the eye and see if she betrayed even a hint of dishonesty or cover-up. Or something, *anything* he could work with. If he woke her out of a sound sleep, so be it. But the porch light was on and from inside, the blueish glow of a TV flickered through the picture window on the right.

So Pags pressed the doorbell and crossed his fingers. The mother was Plan A, B, and C. There was no backup plan.

He didn't get his wish.

Randall Dupree, now sixty-seven and gaunt with disheveled white hair and sunken eyes behind dark-rimmed glasses, answered the door. The years had rendered him a far cry from the robust, middle-aged man who'd left Springvale more than twenty years ago.

Pags had been hoping for the wife, but with no alternatives, he stuck to his plan.

Illuminated by the overhead porch light, he held up his badge, eyes locked onto Randall Dupree, and stood stone still.

Dupree, annoyance initially on his face, blinked once and then twice.

Recognition flashed in his eyes. A guttural gasp escaped from his lips.

"Oh my God," Dupree said, eyes wide, in barely more than a croak. "Not now."

Pags knew that his appearance could also be taken as a notification that tragedy had struck a family member. In fact, that possibility was infinitely more likely than it being tied to the sudden appearance of evidence in a twenty-five-year-old disappearance turned murder. He trusted his instincts that this was the reaction of a guilty man, but if Dupree suffered a heart attack, thinking this visit was about ominous news regarding his son, Pags would never forgive himself and neither would anyone else. It would be Pags's final act on the force, an ignominious end to an honorable career.

So he was quick and clear with his next words.

"We found her body."

Dupree's shoulders slumped in resignation. Defeat filled his eyes.

Pags had been right. His initial gamble had paid off. Now it was time to push all his chips into the middle of the table.

"Why did you do it?" Pags asked.

"How did you find her?" the suddenly very old man asked, his eyes haunted.

Pags ignored the question. He repeated his own while pulling out his smartphone and keying in the number at the station requesting backup, silent approach.

"Why did you do it?" Pags demanded, keeping his eyes locked on Dupree's.

"I had no choice," Dupree said, shaking his head.

Pags gambled again.

"I'm recording this conversation," he said. "You have

the right to remain silent." Pags continued with the rest of the Miranda rights warning while taking hold of Dupree by the elbow and pulling him out onto the porch.

Pags closed the door softly and maneuvered the two of them so he'd be facing the door, just in case the wife made an appearance.

"Why did you have no choice?" Pags asked, trying to get the admission back on track, hoping the rights warning hadn't permanently derailed it but needing to get the words officially on the record.

"You couldn't have waited just two more months," Dupree said wistfully, looking off to the right and shaking his head as if befallen by the worst of luck.

"Two months?" Pags asked.

"I almost made it," Dupree said. "Two months. After all these years. What is it, twenty, twenty-five years? And I missed by two measly months."

"What two months?"

"I have pancreatic cancer," Dupree said. "That's the bad one, not that any of them are good. I only have two months to live. If I'm lucky."

Pags wasn't sure he believed it. The man certainly wasn't getting any sympathy from him even if it was true. But Dupree's gaunt appearance looked even more scarecrow-thin than he'd first appeared in the doorframe.

"I'm sorry to hear that," Pags said, not meaning it for a second but needing to keep the conversation going.

"Just two more months and I could have gone out thinking no one would ever know. Two months! How'd you find the body? Was there DNA?"

Again, Pags responded with a question of his own. "Why did you have no choice?"

"What?" Dupree asked, squinting.

"You said you had no choice. Why did you have no choice?"

"Daniella was pregnant."

Pags suddenly felt a kinship with pancreatic cancer. Whatever it took to rid the world of this piece of vermin.

"Pregnant?"

"I suppose it doesn't matter what I say now," Dupree said. "It's all going to come out."

Pags just nodded.

"All because of two months," Dupree said. "So close." He stared off vacantly.

Pags waited for a time, then broke the silence. "It must have been a shock when she told you."

"She wanted to keep the baby!" Dupree said, still incredulous after all these years. "Can you believe it? She called it our love child. I told her she couldn't, but she didn't understand. It would have ruined me."

Pags thought of Daniella's smiling, fifteen-year-old face that had looked out at him from his computer screen for the last twenty-five years. Sparkling green eyes filled with life and laughter. A pretty smile even with braces covering her every tooth.

Fifteen years old. Still wearing braces. Full of youthful innocence.

Preyed upon by this piece of filth.

Reduced now to a skeleton of dry bones dug up from the ground in broken and mangled pieces. Broken and mangled except for an intact skull still holding most of her teeth. Teeth still encased in corroded braces.

Pags had never once beaten a suspect. It was a line he would not cross. But if ever there was a time for an exception, this was it.

A sour taste filled his mouth. His hands shook.

"You were having an affair with her," Pags said, hating to have to use the neutral term instead of what it really was.

Rape. Statutory rape of a fifteen-year-old. A girl still wearing braces, for the love of God.

"Yeah," Dupree said. "It happened by accident the first time. I was bringing her home from our house one evening—she and Johnny had been studying together or something—and one thing led to another. She was a beautiful child. So beautiful."

Pags tried to calm the rage boiling over inside of him.

"And she was attracted to you?" Pags said, the words searing his brain.

Dupree spread his hands out, palms up, and shrugged.

"I was a rich, powerful man back then," he said. "I wore expensive suits, got expensive haircuts, and drove an expensive car. Young women find that attractive. Maybe because Daniella never knew her father, she was attracted to an older man like me. A father figure. I guess unintentionally, I stole her away from my son."

Pags wanted to tear this man apart, limb from limb, but continued with as calm a demeanor as he could muster.

"But she kept going out with your son?" Pags said.

"She kept up the pretense. It was easier that way. He never knew."

"But then she got pregnant," Pags said.

"I would have lost everything!"

"So what did you do?" Pags asked. "How did you... get rid of her?"

"I picked her up that day with a secret company car I used when I was supposed to be at work but was with her. A black Oldsmobile that was off the books. More discrete than the Mercedes I usually drove." He snorted. "Daniella called it our Love-mobile." A smug look of superiority came over his face. "You never found out about it."

Pags's cheeks burned. "You picked her up at her house? And no one ever saw you?"

"No," Dupree said, the smug look now augmented with a sly grin. "She'd cut through the woods behind her house and meet me in a secluded area where no one would see us."

Dupree fell silent.

"And..." Pags prompted.

"This time, when we finished, I suggested a romantic walk in the woods. She loved the idea! You should have seen her. She was practically beaming."

Should have seen her. Practically beaming.

Pags had no difficulty imagining that. Daniella's smile had beamed at him for twenty-five years. It was a smile he would never forget.

But he had to keep Dupree talking.

"When you... finished?" Pags asked.

"You know."

"Tell me."

"When we finished making love," Dupree said.

Making love.

Pags had all he could do to keep from pulling his service weapon and using it.

"So you… made love with Daniella…" he said as evenly as he could manage. "Then you went for the walk in the woods. Where?" Pags asked.

"To exactly the place where you found her," Dupree said. "So far from any road and so deep into thick woods that I was sure no one would ever find her body. I strangled her, removed her clothing and jewelry to dispose of the next day, threw her in the pit, covered her up, then rushed back into the office—after a change of clothes myself—and made sure I was seen by multiple people working late."

"After digging almost six feet deep?"

Dupree shook his head. "I dug the hole the night before."

Pags was speechless. Premeditated to the first degree. The extent of the man's depravity knew no bounds.

"I was ready with my alibi witnesses and all my answers to your questions carefully rehearsed," Dupree added. "Unlike this time when you ambushed me."

Blue flashers strobed from off to the left as the two backup units Pags had summoned roared up the connecting street and swung around onto Dupree's side street and then into the circular driveway. They skidded to a halt. Four officers came on the run, three men and a woman, weapons drawn.

Pags spun Dupree around and slapped on the handcuffs.

As he did, the front door opened. A short, stout, bleary-eyed woman with her gray hair in curlers—Eileen Dupree—appeared in the doorframe.

"What's going on?" she demanded.

"Your husband is under arrest," Pags said. "We'd like to speak to you, too."

"I'm sorry, Eileen," Randall Dupree said to her. "A long time ago, I did a bad thing."

Pags noticed it was the first time Dupree had expressed any remorse at all. And even this was merely remorse at getting caught. Or at least, at not having succumbed to his cancer before being exposed for what he truly was.

"Officer, let him go!" Eileen Dupree demanded. "He's a very sick man!"

Pags nodded. "Yeah. A very sick man."

STILL AWAKE AT the crack of dawn the next morning, Pags sat alone at his desk in The Closet, the tiny Detectives Room with only six desks, two each against the three facing walls. The smell of his strong coffee filled the room. He'd spent most of the night tying up every last loose end on the case. Now, only one task remained.

Hunting and pecking on his computer keyboard and clicking on the mouse, Pags pulled up the photo of Daniella Cefalo one last time. He would never forget that image. The auburn hair, sparkling green eyes, and the bright smile of a fifteen-year-old girl still wearing braces.

But it was time to remove that photograph from the rotation of images that served as his computer's background wallpaper. Only happy, family photographs would be displayed from now on. He needed no further reminders that his slate was not clean until he brought Daniella the justice she deserved.

Pancreatic cancer might claim Randall Dupree before the justice system, but the man would not go into the ground without the world knowing what he had done.

Without some form of justice served.

Pags sipped his coffee and eyed the retirement paperwork on the upper left corner of his desk. He'd give it a couple more days of thought, but he thought he might just add his signature.

His slate was now clean.

SANTA'S SHRINKAGE

INTRODUCTION TO SANTA'S SHRINKAGE

I've never had more fun writing a story. Readers have told me the feeling is very much mutual.

I wrote "Santa's Shrinkage" for the *2021 WMG Holiday Spectacular*, an advent calendar of sorts for fiction. Subscribers receive in their email inbox a story a day from American Thanksgiving to New Year's Day. The stories fit into one of three genres: crime, romance, or fantasy/science fiction.

I poked around for something unique, as far off the beaten path as possible, and found the Santa Speedo Run. Holy smokes, could anything be more up my alley? I was off and running (pun not intended). As I wrote, I did a bit more poking around and found precisely the other missing piece.

In the end, I didn't just love "Santa's Shrinkage." I didn't just adore it. I wanted "Santa's Shrinkage" to have my babies. (In a literary sense, of course). If the editor of the *Holiday Spectacular*, Kristine Kathryn Rusch, had rejected it, I'd have had to hide all sharp objects in the house.

I didn't have to hide anything.

Kris *loved* the story. She even made it WMG's "Free Story of the Week" to promote the *Holiday Spectacular*. (A helluva promotion if I may discard false modesty and say so myself.) In her introduction, Kris gave my credits, then added the following hilarious comment.

His experience as a runner informs "Santa's Shrinkage." I'm not quite sure if he has other life experiences that inform the non-road-race part of the story.

I doubt he'll tell me, either.

Go ahead and read the story, then come back and read her comment again for another laugh.

Months after the stories appeared in subscribers' email inboxes, WMG collected the crime stories into an anthology titled *Cold-Blooded Christmas*. The following year, Dean Wesley Smith reprinted "Santa's Shrinkage" in *Pulphouse Fiction Magazine*. In his introduction, he complimented my storytelling and wrote that I had "decided to use that amazing skill to tell this very wild story for last year's *Holiday Spectacular*. I knew the minute I read it that the story had to be in these pages."

Yeah, I ain't the only one who loves this story. I hope you join the festive crowd.

SANTA'S SHRINKAGE

I was a dead ringer for Santa. Except for the Speedo.

In theory, I had plenty of competition. Hundreds of us stood packed wall-to-wall inside the Back Bay Social Club, a two-story restaurant and bar on Boylston Street in downtown Boston. During normal dinner hours, well-dressed patrons sit here at tables that extend a couple hundred feet to the rear, the tables covered by crisp white tablecloths. Framed artwork hangs centered on the walls. The polished cherrywood furnishings gleam. With tax and tip, the famous gourmet burger with fries costs thirty dollars.

On this Saturday morning, however, the usual smells have given way to coffee, hot chocolate, and bacon. I bit into another specialty of the house, the donut sandwich, an egg and cheese stacked with mounds of bacon stuffed inside two sugary sweet, glazed donuts. Apparently trying to fatten up those of us who weren't already tipping the scales.

The entire restaurant and bar had been taken over by

five hundred boisterous Santas in Speedos. Mostly bright red Speedos like mine (with a few green ones mixed in), that skimpiest of skimpy, skin-tight, thin-to-the-point-of-near-transparency bathing suit that leaves nothing to the imagination and reveals all. A look that should be reserved for Olympic swimmers.

There weren't many Olympians here.

There were a few chiseled physiques that provided the required exceptions. An astonishing African American bodybuilder. A dozen other workout warriors. Some attractive women in Speedo bikinis catching many a roving eye.

For the most part, though, the acres of bare flesh on display were never going to grace the cover of a fitness magazine. Or any other magazine, for that matter, except as a "before" picture in an advertisement. But since when is Santa supposed to look like Arnold Schwarzenegger? Santa is supposed to be jolly and jumbo sized.

And I was the king of the jumbo-sized Santas. The Ultimate Santa. Not quite fifty years old, I was only five-eight but pushing three hundred pounds. When I walk, I jiggle like a huge lump of Jell-O. My man-boobs are a D cup.

Not the kind of guy you want to see in a Speedo.

But I'll do anything for the right cause. That attitude has brought all of us here for the Santa Speedo Run, held annually two Saturdays before Christmas. It's a one-mile fundraiser for underprivileged Boston area kids, and we're all making a big, loud party out of it.

I'm as much of a party animal as the next guy, and I'm comfortable in my skin. All of it.

Except for *down there*. What's inside my skin-tight Speedo. Or rather, what isn't. Exposed for all the world to see.

On a day like today, size matters.

For some of these guys, the Speedo offers what they consider opportunities for either free advertising or juvenile humor. They've taken markers and scribbled on their stomachs various messages. An arrow pointing downward with phrases like "Jingle Balls" and "Objects below are larger than they appear." Or "Like what you see? Call me," followed by what's either their phone number or the number of someone they truly hate. On their backs, the arrow points downward and the phrase says, "Say yes to crack!"

When it comes to my "package," however, I was not endowed by my creator with a whole lot of endowment. One could say that I have a case of permanent shrinkage. And that's before I venture outside where temperatures today have dropped below freezing.

So I've stuffed a little something extra into my Speedo. The three thick black woolen socks stuffed down there give me the swollen look of a porn star. Hung like a horse. I can barely walk without being bowlegged. Without my something extra, I was bulging out of my Speedo in all the wrong ways. With it, it looks like I've got a howitzer down there.

I've gotten lots of laughs and quips like "Overcompensating?" Each time, I've winked and assured the wise aleck that Mrs. Claus is one satisfied customer. But it's easy being Jolly St. Nick now, here inside in the warmth and comfort of the restaurant. I won't be ho-ho-ho-ing when I step out into the biting cold.

This is my first time participating in the event. And I'm sure it will be my last.

One and done.

WE FILED out into the shockingly frigid weather on Boylston Street, surrounded by a cheering crowd five and six deep. Mostly friends and family, of whom I had none, but also holiday shoppers staring at the unexpected, stunning, and frankly appalling sight. All of them were bundled up in winter coats, scarves, hats, and gloves.

Shivering, I walked to the back of the pack. The two lanes of one-way traffic on Boylston had been blocked off for the start of the event, so the runners stood fifteen or twenty abreast in closely packed rows. But there was no jostling for position. There would be no winners or losers today. No official times.

Not even identifying numbers. We wore only our Speedos, running shoes and socks, a full white Santa beard, and a red-and-white velvet Santa hat. Many had skipped the beard, but not me. Some had replaced the hat with reindeer antlers or added electric Christmas lights draped about their necks. A few of the women and even a couple guys were wearing pink tutus over their Speedos.

A crazy scene.

I wrapped my arms around myself to try to stay warm. Others bounced up and down on their toes. Some, perhaps fueled by a little Irish in their coffee when they were inside, began to sing "Jingle Bells" but with the words changed to "Frozen Balls, Frozen Balls, Frozen All the Way." And then "Deck the Halls with Frozen Balls."

The boisterous laughter and singing continued until finally, somewhere up front, the runners began to chant, "Ten, nine, eight…"

And then we were off. Fenway Park was a mile behind us, the Common a mile ahead, though we'd turn around long before we got there. The Pru—officially known as the Prudential Tower, Boston's second highest skyscraper, fifty floors high—was on our immediate right along with all its associated shops. Further ahead on the right was the Hancock, the one skyscraper to top the Pru, angled to show its wide, blue, checkered face.

On both sides of Boylston were its unique mixture of the old and classic with the new and tacky. The century-old granite edifice of the Boston Public Library on the right, followed on the left by the Old South Church dating back to 1669. Surrounding them were the inevitable Starbucks and Dunks (called Dunkin Donuts only by outsiders), Crate and Barrel, CVS, Verizon, and Lord and Taylor. Atlantic Fish Company, Pizzeria Uno, and the filthy Copley T stop with its subway cars screeching below.

That and the lingering smell of car exhaust.

I huffed and puffed, the plumes of air billowing around me as I chugged along, alternately walking and running. We had long since left the crowd of spectators behind. What remained were mostly random people walking the sidewalks, those sitting in double-parked cars, plus the occasional race-watcher or two every forty or fifty yards, high-fiving the runners. Many looked at me and laughed. Some pointed and shook their heads.

My pride made me hope they were laughing and pointing at my deliberately overstuffed Speedo, not my Santa-esque physique. But who was I fooling? I knew the truth.

And yet it didn't really matter. I was perfectly anonymous. With my full white Santa beard and red-and-white velvet cap, no one could possibly recognize me. Without a single tattoo, visible birthmark, or scar, I was indistinguishable from any other three-hundred-pound fat guy with a flamboyantly fake bulge in his Speedo.

My picture wasn't getting in the newspaper. It had better not. And if it did, who would know it was me? I hadn't even written my real name on the entry form, and I'd paid in cash.

We turned left onto Berkeley then another quick left onto Newbury Street, parallel to Boylston, heading home. Newbury Street was an eight-block, nonstop outdoor mall packed with salons, boutiques, and eateries of all types. Vera Wang Bridal, Ralph Lauren, Hollywood Nails, Sunglass Hut, Tea Forte, Georgetown Cupcakes, Luzzie's Jewelry, art galleries galore, another Starbucks, and Victoria's Secret. And that was just for starters. The variety was endless, almost all of the street's businesses located on the lower floors of four-and-five-story brownstones.

Traffic was no longer blocked off. This was, after all, a long, long cry from the Marathon. The city wasn't shutting down for five hundred Santas in Speedos with almost no spectators other than friends, family, and appalled or comically entertained shoppers. So we ran or walked four and five abreast in the left lane—or in my case, in the back of the pack all by my lonesome—while traffic moved by on the right.

I was freezing my nuts off. My exposed skin had turned red. The frigid cold had wrapped its fist around my bladder and was squeezing. I needed to get this over with and fast. But when I glanced over my right shoulder, I saw a police car slowly driving by with its flashers going. I slowed to a walk, fifty yards behind the nearest pack of slow runners, and the cop passed.

I reached my desired destination—which had never been a rendezvous back at the Back Bay Social Club—and raced across the cobblestone entrance to Luzzies's Jewelry and took the wide, concrete stairs two at a time.

Behind me, a young female voice called out in a joking tone, "Where you going, Santa?"

I did a mental coin flip between "taking a pee"—the first thing that came to mind—and "buying something for Mrs. Claus," and called back over my shoulder with the latter.

The question had apparently come from a redheaded teenage girl I'd just cut past on the sidewalk without even noticing. She laughed, waved, and called out, "Good luck!"

Inside the brightly lit store, the heat hit me like a blast furnace. All my exposed skin suddenly tingled. A perfume-like smell filled the air. A silver crystal chandelier hung overhead, sparkling with what seemed like a hundred tiny, brilliant white lights.

A good-looking couple in their thirties stood hunched over the middle of three polished glass showcases, each almost ten feet wide, this one filled with glittering diamond jewelry. The man was over six feet tall and with short brown hair, the woman of medium height and black hair. Their dark-colored winter coats were draped over their outside arms as they peered in at the diamonds. The clerk helping them, a thin, bald, fiftyish man with dark-rimmed glasses, didn't even look up. Probably close to nailing down a big sale.

"Someone will be out to help you in a second," he said, and pointed to a corner of the showcase.

I reached into my Speedo and whipped it out—one of the three black woolen socks. From inside the sock, I pulled out my custom-made, all-black miniature pistol. Customized to be only a third the size of a regular weapon—even smaller than the Beretta Bobcat 21A mini —it was at the low limit of what could still maintain functionality.

But it worked. Oh baby, it worked. And with a barrel barely more than two inches long, it could be hidden in the palm of my hand. And other strange places.

I clicked off the safety, and chambered the round.

"Put those diamonds in here!" I yelled, my heart racing.

I tossed the sock at the astonished clerk.

"Touch any secret alarms, and it'll be the last sorry thing you do!"

The couple fell back, eyes wide and hands raised. "Don't hurt us!" they cried in unison. Perhaps a good omen for their compatibility. If I didn't have to shoot them. And I wasn't really going to shoot them.

"Is that a *toy*?" the clerk asked, incredulous, staring at the undersized weapon.

This had been a concern all along. The miniature pistol was so small it ran the risk of not being taken seriously. My trigger finger, extended out straight with my other fingers curled around the grip in proper form, could barely fit inside the trigger guard without pulling the trigger.

I didn't want to have to shoot to prove it wasn't a toy. That wasn't part of the plan. But I would if I had to.

"*You want to test me, tough guy*?" I yelled, suddenly sweating so furiously that sweat stung my eyes. "*You feeling lucky? You're going to find out if that sock isn't filled in fifteen seconds!*"

I reached into my Speedo, prompting a shriek from the female customer and a gasp from the clerk. I yanked out another thick, black sock. Tossed it at the clerk.

"*Fill this one, too!*"

I stepped closer. Was only inches from the glittering showcase filled with diamond rings, necklaces, and bracelets. My mouth went dry.

I held the gun pointed steady at the clerk's head. Five feet away.

Then swung it to point at the shrieking couple. Clinging to each other. Terrified.

Then back at the clerk.

"*Twelve seconds! The good stuff or you die!*"

I DASHED OUTSIDE, the frigid cold a hard slap to my sweaty skin. I raced down the stairs and across the cobblestones past a half dozen or so startled passersby.

"Ho, ho, ho!" I called out and turned up Newbury Street. "Merry Christmas!"

They laughed and returned my season's good cheer.

My now even more outrageously overstuffed Speedo held one of the two socks filled by the Luzzie's clerk. I'd stuffed it back in just before leaving the store. The fit, however, was so painful it made my eyes water. The one empty sock I hadn't whipped out and just left in place still protected my so-called family jewels, but imperfectly so. Pointed edges of the stones and jewelry pressed through the woolen material into my member. It was turning my previously lumbering gait into a bowlegged waddle.

My left hand held the other sock half-filled with jewelry. I'd been unable to stuff it back into the Speedo. My right hand cradled the miniature pistol, safety back on, angled in my right palm with my fingers wrapped around the barrel so it was fully concealed but still ready for action.

Before I left, I'd told the clerk and couple inside Luzzie's to sit on the floor and count aloud to one hundred before they moved. And that I'd be coming back to check on them and would shoot anyone who'd disobeyed. Unless the clerk was actually the owner, I thought my chances were decent of them actually waiting until they got to a hundred.

Bowlegged, I ran past Lilly Pulitzer, Bang & Olufsen, and Lush Cosmetics faster than any three-hundred pound Santa with jewelry digging into his nut-sack had a right to do. I took a right onto the Dartmouth Street sidewalk, leaving the official Santa Speedo Run course, and headed for my ten-year-old, unlocked, legally parked black Hyundai.

The foot traffic on these sidewalks was light, and there wasn't a police car in sight. A few parents with children shielded their kids' eyes at my spectacle, but otherwise I was simply the butt of good humor. I could live with that.

Almost home to a rich payday. I could *really* live with that.

I got to within a hundred yards of my car when disaster struck.

The thin fabric of my conspicuously overstuffed Speedo, apparently torn by a jagged edge of some piece of jewelry, gave out.

It split right down the center. Where my supposed howitzer of a male member was supposed to be.

The sock filled with jewelry tumbled onto the sidewalk. Followed by the empty, protective sock.

Leaving only my shrinkage. In the frigid cold.

I fell to my knees and hurriedly stuffed the spillage along with the miniature pistol into the previously empty sock. I looked up and saw two middle-aged African American women heading my way just thirty or forty yards away.

In the distance, a police siren wailed. A cold shiver ran up and down my spine.

I shot to my feet, covered my exposed shrinkage as

best as I could with the three socks, and sprinted for my car.

The women laughed hysterically. As I passed, one of them said, "Oh yeah, I want me some of that!"

They howled with laughter.

More sirens wailed.

I got to the Hyundai—it would have been just my luck if it had been stolen—glanced back and saw that the two women had moved on. None of the other nearby pedestrians could see my split open Speedo and view me as anything other than just another Santa.

I jumped inside and tossed the three socks in an open, black gym bag I'd left on the front seat. I ripped off my Santa hat and beard, stuffed them inside the gym bag, too, and grabbed my car key off the bottom of the bag,

I peeled out of the parking spot.

I pulled an old gray sweatsuit out of the bag and as I drove, pulled on first the sweatshirt with the sweatpants covering my lap, and then, with a bit more difficulty, pulled on the sweat pants left leg first, then the right.

I'd done it!

Pulled off the perfect caper. No one had seen my face or hair. Even back at the Back Bay Social Club. I'd just been the three-hundred-pound Santa with the flamboyant bulge in his Speedo.

Identify that!

I grinned as I imagined the two women who'd seen my shrinkage asking for a six-pack of crotch shots for comparison. Not happening! Or a court case where a witness was asked to identify me only to have him or her admit, "I was looking, um, *down there*."

I'd need to be careful fencing the jewelry, of course, and I'd be ditching the Santa garb and the ruined Speedo in a McDonald's trash receptacle soon. But I was home free.

It had been the perfect crime.

Had I been a bit of a Grinch taking advantage of this run for charity? Hey, those underprivileged kids were still getting my entry fee, just like from all the other participants. I'd merely made this particular event also a fundraiser for my own retirement.

And a big thank you to Luzzie's Jewelry for its generous donation!

As for all of those laughing at me in my Speedo, hey, I can take a joke. I also got the last laugh. Sometimes shrinkage can work to a guy's advantage. There are worse things than being endowed by your creator with a tiny endowment.

CHIMICHANGAS AND A
COUPLE OF GLOCKS

INTRODUCTION TO CHIMICHANGAS AND A COUPLE OF GLOCKS

Michael Bracken is one of the most revered names in crime short fiction, both as a writer and editor. He's won the Edward D. Hoch Memorial Golden Derringer Award for lifetime achievement in short mystery fiction along with countless other honors. So when he came calling with an opportunity to contribute a novelette/novella in his *Guns & Tacos* series, I jumped.

Over the years, I've gotten to know many editors and can call them friends, close friends in many cases. At the time, however, I only knew Michael Bracken from afar. He'd bought my story "Sneaker Wave" for the inaugural volume of his *Mickey Finn: 21st Century Noir* series, we'd met briefly at a World Mystery Convention (aka Boucheron), and seen each other's comments within the Short Mystery Fiction Society discussion group. But I doubt he could have picked me out of a lineup, and I certainly wasn't a regular contributor to his many projects. As a result, I considered it a special honor that he selected me for one of the series' six annually available slots.

Each episode of the *Guns & Tacos* series revolves around a taco truck in Chicago known for its daily specials. Late at night and during the wee hours of the morning, it isn't the food selection that attracts customers, it's the illegal weapons available with the special order.

A unique and fascinating springboard for a story.

I began with the Lizzie character—for me, it almost always begins with the main character—and then from her to Peter and their relationship. At some point, a friend's odd, unsettling experience at a bar came to mind and from there, the pieces to the puzzle fell into place.

CHIMICHANGAS AND A COUPLE OF GLOCKS

Peter looked terrified and he *never* looked like that. That scared the living daylights out of Lizzie Hosker. In the eight months she'd known him, and the four months they'd lived together, she'd never seen him even the least bit frightened. He was always cocky as hell with his thick, dark hair, his muscular build, and blue eyes. His snug designer jeans and dress shirts fit him just right, the top three buttons on his shirts left unbuttoned to show a thin, gold chain nestled in his black chest hair.

Cocky, always. And why wouldn't he be? Frightened, never.

Lizzie knew what other people thought when they saw the two of them together: *what the hell does he see in her?* He had the movie star good looks and the bright smile; she was Plain Jane. Scrawny, barely five feet tall, flat-chested, and mousy. Drab, brown hair that just hung there, not quite to her shoulders. Boring brown eyes. As glamorous as cardboard. Yet they were engaged to be married. The ultimate odd couple.

She sat at the circular kitchen table, facing the apartment's front door, her textbooks fanned out in a semicircle atop the plain white tablecloth, her laptop centered in the middle. A junior year pre-med at the University of Chicago, she was studying for her Pathogenic Bacteriology and Immunology exam next week. It was the first week of October, a month into what UC referred to as the Autumn Quarter, and she already knew the textbook inside and out, had her notes memorized, and was at least a week ahead in all of her other studies. But you could never be too prepared.

The smell of garlic bread and lasagna—Peter's favorite—filled the kitchen, emanating from the oven behind her. To her left, the refrigerator hummed beside a sink and stove. Though she'd been a vegetarian for years prior to meeting Peter, she made the lasagna with sweet Italian sausage because that was how he liked it.

And what Peter liked, Peter got. She couldn't even pick out the pieces of sausage in her own slice of lasagna. The one time she'd tried that had infuriated Peter, and he'd made her pay. It had been painful to sit for a week.

Never again.

So tonight she would follow all his rules to the letter, eat the pieces of meat, smile at the right time, laugh at his jokes, and maybe for a change they could actually *make love*, not that other stuff. Actually kiss and share nice romantic gestures like in the movies, like she'd heard people engaged to be married did.

Not that other stuff.

A girl could dream, couldn't she?

But all such dreams flew out the window when Peter

burst through the front door and slammed it behind him. Lizzie looked up and tried her prettiest smile, knowing full well it really wasn't pretty at all. But it was the best she had.

Her painfully ordinary smile faltered, then was gone.

Peter was in trouble. *Big* trouble. Had to be. His eyes were wild, his breathing ragged. Beads of sweat formed on his forehead as he stood across the table from her.

"What's wrong?" Lizzie cried, trying to get to her feet but falling back into her chair, her legs suddenly weak.

"You've got to help me," Peter said, and took a big gulp of air. "I've got a...got an *emergency*. You gotta help."

Was it money again? Peter always needed money. He was *always* broke, and it was always an emergency. She paid for everything. The apartment. The food. The last four payments on his Acura. He would say he needed the money, she would pay, and that was that. It was, she thought, an investment in their future together.

But the requests for money—that somewhere in the back of her mind she acknowledged were actually demands—had never come like this. Not with panicked eyes. Or rasping breath. Or such obvious fear. At least no fear on *his* part. He would smile and ask nicely, cajoling her, laying on the charm, pointing out that eventually when that diamond ring she wore—a ring she'd also paid for, though she would deny that humiliating fact to her dying day—when it was joined by a wedding ring, their money would all be shared anyway. So what difference did it make?

He'd be sweet, or at least as sweet as Peter ever got. Not frightened like this.

"What trouble are you in?" Lizzie asked.

Peter shook his head. "Better you didn't know."

"Peter, you're scaring me," Lizzie said, her heart pounding even harder than when Peter made his other demands.

He stepped to the table, reached across it, and grabbed her by the shoulders. Tight. So tight it hurt.

"You need to do this," he said, shaking her. "Now put on your big girl pants and listen to me."

Lizzie nodded. Tears pooled in her eyes, but she held them back, blinking rapidly. Peter hated when she cried at times like these. Crying was only for their *playtime*, as he called it.

"There's a truck where you're going to pick up something for me," Peter said, his eyes trying to lock onto hers even as she looked away. "*Look at me!*" he roared, and pulled back a strong, hard hand to hit her.

"No!" she yelped. "I mean, yes!"

Lizzie looked into Peter's dark, cold eyes. She thought they were like a serpent's eyes. Her chest thundered. She tried to breathe, but couldn't.

"Okay, now," Peter said, lowering his hand. He exhaled noisily through his nose, then ran his fingers through his hair. "You're going to pick up a package for me."

Lizzie wanted to cry. "*Drugs?*"

"No, not drugs, you stupid bitch!" Peter said with a shake of his head.

Lizzie hated when he called her a bitch, but at least it wasn't the C word. And of course, calling her a stupid bitch didn't make any sense, not when she had a 4.0 GPA in pre-med, and he was barely staying afloat in Business Management. He didn't apply himself. Skipped too many classes. But she knew she couldn't say a word of that in reply. She'd better not let even the hint of the thought cross her face.

So she just looked at him, trying desperately to keep her face blank.

"It's something to protect me," Peter said.

"Protect you?"

"*Is there a fucking echo in here?*"

Lizzie shook her head furiously. She couldn't imagine what trouble Peter was in or what she might get to protect him, but she'd learned long ago, long before she even met Peter, to do what she was told and keep her mouth shut.

"Okay," Peter said. "It's going to cost several hundred dollars. Maybe even close to a thousand. So bring a thousand just in case. Cash."

"A thousand dollars?" Lizzie asked, the words slipping out before she could stop them. "Peter, what is happening? What do you need a thousand dollars for to protect you?"

Anger filled Peter's eyes. Lizzie cringed. She was sure she was going to pay for not keeping her mouth shut. But this time she got lucky. He just shook his head and replied through clenched teeth.

"This is to keep me alive. Do you think I'm worth it, or is that too much for you?"

"Of course! I'm sorry." Lizzie swallowed hard. "What do I need to do?"

"You're going to go find this truck and a guy named

Jesse. Sometime after ten tonight. Between ten and four in the morning."

"Four in the morning?" Lizzie felt her eyes widen, despite her best attempts not to show any reaction. She had an eight a.m. class, though she certainly couldn't say that. Couldn't even think it and was ashamed of herself for doing so. This was her fiancée! Her future husband! How could she even think about her classes and being tired and preserving her perfect 4.0 GPA? This was to keep Peter alive. She was such a horrible, horrible person. She deserved every last punishment he meted out on her.

"And it's...it's not going to be in a good part of town," Peter said, fortunately not reading her thoughts.

"Where?" Lizzie asked, holding her breath.

"Somewhere near Fuller Park."

Ooof! The words came as a slap, every bit as hard as the ones he applied to her bottom during *playtime*. Lizzie almost wet her pants. Fuller Park was the most dangerous part of Chicago. The murder capital of the city. She'd never once dared to step foot even close to it.

"*Fuller Park?*" she said feebly, knowing she should keep her big mouth shut but unable to help herself.

"Yeah, you're going to do it, and you aren't going to be a baby about it!"

Lizzie nodded, trying to look brave, trying to feel brave, but failing on all counts. Her mind raced. *Fuller Park, Fuller Park, Fuller Park!* And then, *between ten at night and four in the morning! In Fuller Park!* She couldn't breathe. Couldn't swallow. Finally, she managed, "What kind of truck?"

"A taco truck," Peter said.

Lizzie stared at him for a moment, not comprehending, and then it hit her. *A taco truck!* Relief washed over her. All the tension and fear that had been tightening and tightening like a clenched fist burst free. *Taco truck!* She had all she could do to keep from bursting out in laughter. Only the memory of what had happened the last time Peter thought she was laughing at him stopped her.

But it was hard to hold back the belly laugh. All this talk of taking a thousand dollars into Fuller Park—*a thousand dollars into Fuller Park in the dead of night!*—and Peter's Oscar-worthy performance of fearing for his life, it had all been nothing more than an elaborate ruse to again bring up her big mistake. To again pressure her for a threesome.

"Is that all this is?" she asked. "You're just teasing me about tacos again?"

The word "taco" had caused so much pain between the two of them. Well, had caused so much pain for *her*. Peter called it teasing, and she tried to convince herself that that's all it was, but it was tormenting, no doubt about it. He knew it and she knew it.

He'd had to explain it to her at first. A "sausage fest" was a party where there were almost all guys; a "taco fest" was one were there were almost all women. Even then, she still hadn't gotten it. Her, a 4.0 pre-med student. He'd had to connect the dots. Penis to sausage; vulva—or as he put it, "pussy"—to taco.

She'd felt her face redden at the explanation back then and even more when he continually rubbed her nose in it, reminding her—ridiculing her—for that *one time*, for that *one mistake*. For the one time she'd "gone taco." Been with a woman.

Even though it really had been his fault.

THE NIGHT that ended their relationship, though not forever, Lizzie thought they were having sex in their normal way. Which was anything but normal, but was normal for her and Peter. Giving him what he wanted, what he needed. And maybe she needed it, too, although she felt so perpetually conflicted and guilty about sex that she really wasn't sure what she wanted or what she needed.

It had been that way since she was eleven when Uncle Bob did those things to her. Touching her in her private, dirty places. Then blaming her and threatening to tell her parents if she said a word to anyone.

And when she did remain silent, he did even more things.

For three years.

Until her mother caught the two of them.

And though her mother did threaten to cut Uncle Bob's penis off with a steak knife, she saved the lion's share of the blame for Lizzie. *How could you let a man do that to you? Why did you tempt Uncle Bob, who is a church-going, God-fearing man, with a wife and three kids of his own! What kind of a shameful* slut *are you to have done all of that? What is* wrong *with you?*

Lizzie had been trying to figure out what was wrong with her ever since.

In quiet. That was the ironclad rule, back then and to this day. No one else was to know. Not her father. Not Uncle Bob's wife. There was no need to ruin his marriage. No need to cast shame on her three cousins when she, Lizzie, was the one to blame. No one was to know! And certainly no therapist, a stranger for God's sake!

She was to keep her mouth shut, her legs closed, and stop looking and acting like a whore. Maybe then, if she was lucky, no one else but the three of them would ever find out about the terrible things she had done. No one else would have to know what a horrible little girl she was. What a tramp. An embarrassment to herself and to her family and to all of God's creation.

Perhaps, if she told no one, she could even forget it herself. Pretend it had never happened. Make sure nothing like it ever happened again. She wouldn't even *dare* to look pretty and seduce an innocent man. Look as ugly as she could, stay away from all boys, and certainly all men, so she would never tempt them again. And maybe if it never happened again, her horrible secret would be buried like a decaying corpse and no one would ever have to know that it was even there. That it had ever been there.

Not even she would remember.

So Lizzie kept her mouth shut and tried to bury it. But her shameful secret crawled out of the moist earth like a decaying corpse from the horror movies to remind her what a horrible person—what a sinful, shameful, depraved little girl who didn't deserve to live—she was.

Over and over. The decaying corpse of her secret crawled out and pointed a skeletal finger at her. She was just a shameful slut. A tramp who had tricked a married man, her uncle, into having sex with her.

She was a horrible, horrible person, no matter how many straight-A report cards she got. No matter that she made herself as unattractive as possible. No matter that she made absolutely sure she didn't accidentally seduce any married men. No matter that she didn't date any boys, ever.

She was a horrible person and always would be. That skeletal finger would forever point at her and remind her of her shame.

Until Peter.

Peter saw something in her that first day at the library. And he told her she was pretty! Lizzie was sure he was mocking her. Of course, he was mocking her. Boys had been doing that for years.

And even if Peter wasn't, Lizzie didn't want to be pretty. She wasn't supposed to be pretty. Pretty was what had ruined her life.

But Peter persisted. He wasn't mocking her. He told her she really was pretty! And he could release that inner beauty of hers if only she would let him.

The beauty of pain, he told her on their third date. Punishing what was bad inside her—and *so much* was bad inside her!—so she could be free.

He could make her happy. Through *playtime*. Sometimes he called it *pain-time*. He could grant her freedom through pain.

Perhaps, Lizzie told herself, every punishment was beating that decaying corpse and its accusatory skeletal finger. Beating the corpse into submission even as she submitted to Peter's hand.

The theory was working, at least as well as any theory had worked for Lizzie, until the night two months ago, two months after Peter had moved in with her, when it almost ended forever.

It had begun with the usual spanking. Sometimes, Peter preferred that she wear her tightest pair of jeans and the spanking would start that way. More often, though, he preferred a dress, and that was the case that night. He sat on their queen-sized, four-poster bed, the walnut headboard to his left, the matching dressers to his right. Nightstands with lamps turned down low, but not off, bracketed the two sides of the bed. The woody, musky scent of sex candles filled the air.

Peter pulled up her dress, bent her over his lap, and began to spank, first with her underwear still on, then with it pulled down. As his palm slapped harder and harder, and the stinging of her bottom hurt more and more, Peter told her what an awful, shameful slut she was —reminding her what she already knew, what she could never forget—but by taking her punishment, she was becoming beautiful.

Then he took off all her clothes, applied a black satin blindfold and a cloth gag, and threw her onto the bed, calling her "his dirty slut," which was surely true. He tied her wrists and ankles tightly to the four posts with the well-worn, clothesline-thick rope he always used. She yelped with the pain she knew she deserved with every pinch of her nipples and every slap of her inner thighs.

She groaned in the way she knew Peter liked when he played with her down there.

Then came the hot wax from the candles. Not ordinary candles, of course, which would leave second-degree burns and could send someone to the hospital. Peter wasn't an animal. He also wasn't a novice. He knew what he was doing. And as each drop splattered onto her skin, hurting terribly but the pain so very much deserved and really not that much more intense than the rest of their repertoire, Peter repeated his mantra.

"Take it, you dirty bitch! Take it!"

Nothing at all out of the ordinary. Just what Lizzie had come to expect. Giving Peter what he needed. Taking whatever he decided to give her, whatever he decided she needed.

After a short break, during which the hot wax hardened and she grew more and more nervous, wondering what would happen next, Peter began taking photographs with what sounded like his iPhone. Lizzie didn't like that. If he ever got tired of her—a frightening possibility she had to at least consider even though they were engaged—he might not want to give the photographs back. He'd taken photos before, but when she protested nicely afterwards, had promised he'd deleted them.

But here he was taking photographs again. A *lot* of them.

Click! Click! Click! Click!

Lizzie shook her head in protest—something she never did—but Peter seemed to take the photos even faster.

Click! Click! Click! Click! Click! Click! Click! Click!

Impossibly fast.

Click! Click! Click! Click! Click! Click! Click! Click! Click! Click! Click! Click!

She shook her head more forcefully.

"Do what I say!" he commanded.

And then he took off the blindfold.

There, hovering over her, taking pictures with their phones, were three other men at the foot of the bed. Strangers she had never seen before.

Pants and underwear either down at their ankles, or off entirely, Lizzie couldn't see.

Fully erect.

Lizzie screamed through her wet cloth gag.

"She's all yours, boys," Peter said with a smile and a gleam in his eyes.

"No!" Lizzie screamed through the gag. She shook her head fiercely from side to side. *"NO!"*

One of them hesitated. He had short blond hair and tattoos all across his chest and upper arms.

"You said she wanted this!" he said to Peter.

"She does!" Peter said, eyes wild.

He turned to Lizzie, grabbed her chin tightly, and said, "Tell them you really want it!"

But *no, no, no,* she couldn't do that. She may be a horrible person and a shameful slut—she was!—but she couldn't do that!

Lizzie shook her head *no, no, no.* As best she could through the cloth gag, she tried to scream, *"Rape!"*

As the other two strangers stood there, saying noth

ing, looking at each other, the blond grabbed Peter and shoved him.

"What the fuck are you trying to do? Set us up to go to jail for life?"

"No, she wants it!" Peter said.

The blond man narrowed his eyes. "Let's see."

When he loosened the knot on the back of the gag and it fell free, Lizzie let loose a blood-curdling scream that left no doubt.

"You fucking asshole!" the naked blond man said, getting his face right in Peter's. "You fucking asshole!"

"She said this was what she wanted," Peter said, spreading his hands wide, a look of innocence on his face even as Lizzie demanded to be set free. Peter clamped a hand down on her mouth. "She's been talking about it for weeks. This was her secret fantasy she wanted to come true. Swear to God! She must have changed her mind."

LIZZIE STAYED the next three nights in a tiny studio apartment with an old classmate named Julie O'Meara. Average height and shape, Julie had curly, light-brown hair, brown eyes, and had always been friendly with a warm smile back when they took classes together freshman year. They'd never been close friends—Lizzie didn't do that close friends sort of thing—and they'd barely seen each other after Julie dropped out of pre-med and shifted to something less demanding. But Julie's was the first familiar face Lizzie bumped into after fleeing her apartment barefoot, hair askew, tears streaming down her face, and blouse misbuttoned.

Lizzie told Julie nothing of what had just happened—old habits die hard, even the worst of them—only that she needed a place to stay for a couple nights. Lizzie offered to sleep on the floor—there was only the tiny bedroom, bathroom, and kitchen—but Julie insisted that they could squeeze into her twin bed, and they did. Lizzie did her best not to disrupt her host's sleep, fighting off the urge to break into a crying jag and trembling fits that might never end.

On the second night, Lizzie lay in bed beneath the covers, eyes closed, her back flat against the wall so she'd take up as little space on the tiny bed as possible, and counted silently down from a hundred to try to calm her breathing and hold off the urge to cry.

She felt soft lips upon hers. Gently kissing her.

Lizzie's eyes shot open wide. Her whole body became rigid. "*What are you doing?*"

"Shhh!" Julie said, and held a finger to Lizzie's lips.

"I'm not—"

"Something's wrong, I can tell. Let me make you feel better," Julie said.

Lizzie didn't move. This wasn't her. She wasn't a lesbian. She was sure of it. She was all kinds of awful things. Her mother had been right about them all. And being a lesbian wouldn't be awful at all. Especially after what had just happened. She never wanted to see a man again.

But she wasn't a lesbian.

Still, Lizzie didn't want to seem rude to her host. And maybe she could learn to be a lesbian.

And never have a man in her life again. Never a man like Peter. The thought of him made her shudder, which Julie took as encouragement. Never men like those three strangers who, all but her blond rescuer, were going to follow Peter's biding and prove once and for all—if it ever needed proof—what a shameful, worthless, filthy slut Lizzie really was.

She shuddered again.

Julie moved lower until her kisses were *down there.* Tender kisses. Something totally unfamiliar to Lizzie.

Oooh-boy. Lizzie didn't know what to think. Except that she didn't deserve this.

It was too... too loving. *Loving?* Sensual without being painful.

No, she certainly didn't deserve this. She was a totally worthless piece of dung. Deserving of nothing but getting her bottom whipped. Her mother had been right about everything. Heck, Lizzie had almost seduced three strangers into gang-raping her. What more proof was needed?

But Julie was... *oooh-boy.*

Oooh-boy.

Oooh-boy.

After a lot of *oooh-boys,* Lizzie guiltily tried to reciprocate. Though Julie told her to take this slow, that would be for another night, Lizzie knew she didn't deserve to be on the receiving end of pleasure. That only proved her mother had been right. And Lizzie certainly couldn't take and not give back. That was being the most wanton slut of all.

She was supposed to give pleasure, not take it. Like she'd given so much to Peter so many times. Not receiving pleasure except in pain.

So she tried to give pleasure to Julie, and though Julie responded with encouraging moans, it still felt all wrong to Lizzie. She just wasn't wired that way. She could force herself to do it, like she forced herself to do things for Peter. But this just wasn't her.

Lizzie heard her mother's accusing voice. First, Uncle Bob, a God-fearing, married man with three kids. Then three men ready to ravish her all at the same time. Now with a woman. *Enjoying it with a woman.* Sodom and Gomorrah had nothing over the wanton whore that Lizzie had become.

PETER FOUND out about the episode on their sixth day back together. And never let her forget it.

Lizzie hadn't intended to reconcile with him. She'd blocked his repeated calls, first on his regular phone and then what must be a burner. She wanted no part of him ever again. The horror of those three strangers standing beside the bed, prepared to... prepared to...

Ooof!

Lizzie shuddered as she walked down the suddenly long, fourth-floor halfway to her apartment door on the left. *Yea though I walk through the valley of the shadow of death* flashed through her mind. She didn't want to be here. Didn't want to think about what had happened in that apartment bedroom. Didn't want to recall Peter's words urging the strangers on.

She never wanted to see Peter again.

But she had to get her things. She could replace her clothes. Might actually want to burn anything Peter had touched. But she needed her heavily highlighted textbooks and her laptop, which held all her detailed notes. There was only so much she'd been able to do at the library and on its computers. It was amazing she'd lasted almost three days without her books and laptop.

If only she'd been able to grab them as she fled the scene that night. Then she'd never need to return to the apartment again. Get the lease cancelled and never step foot in *the valley of the shadow of death*. But she'd had all she could do to throw on her clothes and run like hell barefoot from Peter and those men.

There was nothing fortunate about that night with the three strangers. Nothing. Except of course that the blond one had refused to...refused to...

Ooof!

Lizzie shuddered again. She tried to push that image if not away—those things never, ever truly left—but push it into that buried deep part of her mind with Uncle Bob and...

Ooof! Go away!

Lizzie tried to clear her thoughts. At least that awful night—*ooof! ooof! ooof!*—at least it had happened on a Friday so she'd had no classes the next two days. But now it was Monday morning and she had no choice but to retrieve her books and laptop.

With any luck, Peter wouldn't be here. Or at least he'd be sleeping so soundly he wouldn't hear her—it was barely after six in the morning—and she could grab her things. He'd never know she'd been there. As long as she had her books and laptop, she could find somewhere else to stay. Maybe she could even go back to Julie and learn to be a lesbian. Lizzie doubted it, but maybe she hadn't given it enough time.

No, she'd just find another apartment. She did have *some* money left. Her parents had both passed away in recent years, and as an only child, she'd inherited what little there was to inherit. But Peter had been plowing through that money at an alarming rate. It wouldn't last forever. And unfortunately, the apartment was in her name, and it had been her security deposit. If Peter trashed the place, she'd be responsible for it.

She had to kick Peter out, didn't she? And how could she ever do that? She'd never ordered him to do anything. And if he refused, which of course he would, then what could she do? She wasn't about to call the police and have to explain what had happened.

What a mess she'd made. And of course, she deserved it all. Awful things happened to awful people.

Holding her breath, Lizzie turned the key in the lock. The clicking sound roared in her ears. It echoed down the cavernous, empty hallway. She tiptoed inside.

She let her eyes adjust to the dim light, the darkness broken only by the early morning sunlight streaming in the six-foot-wide living room window on the right.

Peter was in the apartment—of course he was!—sleeping in the bedroom off to the back left, its door wide open. Lizzie listened to his slight snore. Perhaps she might get lucky after all and pull off a clean getaway. In and out of the apartment in less than five minutes, with Peter never knowing she'd even been here.

But since when did Lizzie Hosker ever get lucky? When did it ever make sense for her to hope for anything? Her books and laptop were nowhere to be found.

Of course.

They'd been on the circular kitchen table when she'd fled—*for her life!*—on Friday night. Now, she tiptoed through the kitchen, checking the cabinets, atop the refrigerator, even somewhat absurdly, in the oven. Then through the living room, beneath and behind the couch, on the coffee table, and then...

Into the windowless bedroom. Darker than the rest of the apartment.

Where Peter still slept, smelling of alcohol, though no longer snoring, on the four-poster bed. Where the three strangers had stood around her as she lay there helpless...

Ooof!

Lizzie's heart jackhammered. She fought back a jagged cry. Held her breath. And got down on all fours to look under the bed. At first, it was too dark to see, but then in the shadows more than an arm's length away...

Jackpot!

Three stacks of books and, to their left, the laptop.

Holding her breath, Lizzie flattened herself against the carpet. She reached far beneath the bed, just barely touching the first stack. As silently as she possible, she slowly slid it toward her.

Got it.

Two more to go plus the laptop. Her nose began to twitch with the dust she'd raised, so she opted to get the laptop next. Just in case she had to make a run for it. The laptop with all her notes and completed assignments was the top priority. If she'd been thinking, she would have gotten it first, but who could think at times like this? She got it out, though, and was reaching for the next stack when a strong, warm hand touched the back of her neck.

Lizzie screamed.

The hand's grasp tightened for an instant, then released its grip.

"Why don't you answer my calls?" Peter asked.

Lizzie lay there unmoving. Unable to speak.

"You treat me like I'm a monster," he said.

And you are! Lizzie thought, but certainly couldn't say it. She swallowed hard and just lay there. Helpless again. Such a familiar feeling.

"I was only doing what I thought you wanted," Peter said, calmly and reasonably. Like a stockbroker describing investments. "Everything we've always done has been to give you what you want. Give you what you need."

What I want? What I need? How could you ever think that's what I wanted?

But again, she couldn't speak the thoughts aloud. Only lay there, his firm hand still upon the back of her neck, holding her down but only loosely. The rough fabric of the carpet scratched her nose. Its slight musty scent filled her nostrils.

"I only wanted to please you," Peter said. "It was the logical next step."

Please me?

"I love you, Lizzie."

THE MAKEUP SEX almost made her late for her nine o'clock class. She'd been such a fool to think that Peter would have forced the three men on her if he hadn't truly thought that had been what she secretly wanted.

In fact, he had to punish her for even thinking that of him. And for thinking he would allow those three men to leave the apartment without deleting their photos of her. What kind of monster did she think he was? So many evil thoughts of her to punish! So many punishments that she deserved.

The makeup sex resumed that night after dinner at Ruth's Chris Steak House on North Dearborn. Lizzie paid with her credit card, of course, since Peter had no money. And most vegetarians, even lapsed ones, preferred other restaurants than steak houses.

But it was the thought that counted. And the thoughts of hers that required atonement. She definitely deserved the extra-hard spankings that night and the tight nipple clamps.

But Peter really sealed the deal the next night when he got down on one knee and proposed, albeit with a ring from a bubble gum machine.

"We are so right for each other," he said. "I want to spend the rest of my life with you and only you. Will you marry me?"

Shocked—*stunned!*—Lizzie said yes. Of course, she said yes!

Two nights later, they went shopping for a real ring, a half-carat diamond. Lizzie felt euphoric, even as she signed the credit card slip.

That night, Peter tied her up face down and gave Lizzie what she truly deserved. But with extra lube, of course.

On the weekend, while bent over Peter's lap getting spanked, she let slip about her experience with Julie.

"Were you with any other men while we were apart?" Peter asked, his breathing heavy.

Lizzie, who could never be a poker player because she was the worst liar in the world, said no, but something in her voice betrayed her.

"*Lizzie?*" he asked, and brought his hand down hard.

Peter got the truth out of her minutes later.

"You taco-loving slut!" he said gleefully.

Peter had been tormenting her as a "taco lover" ever since—"Lizzie the Lesbo!"—along with demands that she set up a "taco party" for him, a threesome with her and Julie. Or a suitable substitute.

Lizzie always gave in to Peter's demands. Always. But their agreement even before their engagement, their agreement even as she lay face down on the bedroom floor with Peter's hand on her neck and the carpet fabric scraping her nose, was that there would be no one else. He could have his way with her and give her what punishments he wanted—"what you need!" he had said—but never again would there be anyone else in the bedroom with them.

Even she had her limits. No three strangers. No Julie, or anyone else.

She was not Lizzie the Lesbo, no matter what Peter said. Though that didn't stop him from bringing up her "love for tacos" and the possibility of a "taco party" for him on an almost daily basis.

So two months later, relief washed over her after Peter scared the living daylights out of her with his talk of him being in grave danger only to have it be nothing more than an elaborate gag to once again torment her about her mistake.

Taco truck!

Peter being Peter. Lizzie just wondered about the exact term. If a taco party was multiple women, then what was a taco truck? Big women?

But, no, it turned out that a taco truck really meant... a taco truck.

LIZZIE GRIPPED the ten-year-old Hyundai's steering wheel so tightly her knuckles turned white. Her heart jackhammered, threating to explode out of her chest. She tried to swallow but couldn't. Felt a bitter taste in her mouth and down her throat.

Ooof! Fuller Park! And in the pitch black darkness of midnight, no less. With fifteen hundred dollars in her pocket—Peter had told her a thousand, but she'd brought extra, just in case—practically asking to be robbed and even worse. Why weren't there more working streetlights? Fuller Park had a scary reputation even in broad daylight. Darkness made it even more menacing. She'd never once stepped foot in the neighborhood and had intended to always keep it that way.

It wasn't Fuller Park's racial makeup. It was all the murders. And here she was—she, who hardly ever ventured outside of her apartment and the UC campus—driving through it in the dead of midnight.

Dead was what she'd be lucky not to be an hour from now. Or maybe she might even be wishing she were dead. *Ooof!* She checked that the car doors were locked for perhaps the tenth time as she drove by seven or eight young men sitting on the stoop of yet another boarded-up house.

Lizzie held her breath and kept driving, looking straight ahead even while checking with her peripheral vision to make sure that no one was running at the car from the side. Ready to smash in the windows and drag her from the car.

Ooof!

House after house was boarded up, their small yards overrun with knee-high weeds. Graffiti covered the walls of abandoned warehouses. More streetlights were burned out or broken, giving the orange glow cast by those that worked an even more haunting look.

The fifteen hundred dollars in her pocket burned.

Why couldn't Peter do this himself? He was the bold, brave one; she was the timid mouse. And this was even worse for a woman. She didn't even want to think about what could happen. An image flashed before her eyes of the two strangers in her bedroom that night who would have followed Peter's urging if not for her blond defender.

Ooof! Where had that come from? She'd buried that memory two months ago. What was it doing springing up at a time like this? When she was already so scared—so terrified!—she was about to pee her pants and could barely hold back tears that would certainly gush forth if she let loose the dam.

She pushed the memory aside. Buried it back where it belonged. And tried to stop thinking about how this was more dangerous for a woman, and how Peter really hadn't asked, he'd demanded. She'd had no choice. But when did she ever have a choice? Not that she was complaining. Although, she knew she was. She didn't want to be here. Wanted to get out of here as fast as possible.

Guilt washed over her. How could she be so selfish? Peter, her fiancée, the man with whom she was going to spend the rest of her life, was in desperate trouble, and she was complaining about helping him? What was wrong with her? She should *want* to help him. She should be ready to do whatever it took to help him.

Even if she was just a mouse. It was time for this mouse to have a backbone and be there for her man.

But why did she have to be a mouse? Why were her proverbial whiskers always twitching with fear?

Where was the stupid taco truck? And why couldn't it drive to a safer neighborhood? Heck, it was a truck! Why couldn't it do deliveries? Be the Dominoes of tacos! And whatever else "the special" entailed.

Her palms moist, Lizzie squeezed the Hyundai's steering wheel even harder, wondering if it was possible for it to crack and fall apart at the hands of a twig like herself. Wouldn't that be how her luck ran! Have the car break down in this neighborhood even though she serviced it precisely on time, even down to oil changes every three thousand miles.

Get me out of here!

And then suddenly, miraculously, as if in answer to prayer—though she'd stopped believing in such a thing about a decade ago—the form of a white truck appeared in the distance, parked beneath the hazy, orange glow of a sodium streetlight.

Strains of the Hallelujah Chorus played in Lizzie's mind, mocking her to be sure, but she thought she just might get out of this alive.

As she pulled up behind the vehicle, she saw that it was battered and old, maybe even older than she was. At some point in the distant past, the sign on the rear had read JESSE'S TACOS in thick, foot-high black letters against the white background. But the first E and the O were now little more than smudges, making it J SSE'S TAC S.

Who would actually eat at a place like this? The smells in the air of fried beef, chicken, and pork might have their allure for non-vegetarians, not to mention the fried corn tortillas, but what hit her nose hardest was the distinctly unappetizing smell of grease. *Eeew, gross!* Then again, she wasn't here for the food.

Seeing no customers around—no surprise there—and no other lurking threats, Lizzie took a deep breath, patted the money split evenly in her two pants pockets, tried unsuccessfully to calm her pounding heart, and got out of the car.

A huge, middle-aged black man waited for her at the truck's service window, his hands resting on the counter, leaning forward. Lizzie didn't follow sports, but she guessed he might have played for the Bears years ago at one of the positions that hit other players and hit them hard. He had to be six-five or taller, and close to three hundred pounds.

Though the night had turned a bit cold after unseasonably warm days in the sixties and even low seventies, so Lizzie was wearing her navy blue coat, the hulking form looming over her wore nothing more on his upper half than a sleeveless, white undershirt she'd heard called a wifebeater. Tattoos covered every inch of his massive, heavily muscled arms, and every inch of his neck. There was even a tattoo of a tear leaking from his right eye.

Lizzie gulped. "Are you Jesse?"

"Yeah, I'm Jesse."

Lizzie thought if she ever got a tattoo—which she never, ever would; she felt squeamish just thinking about it, but if she did—that tear tattoo would be right for her. She should have tattoos of hundreds of tears streaming down her face. That would be a Lizzie tattoo.

But maybe Jesse's tear tattoo wasn't supposed to

symbolize crying. He looked like he'd never cried once in his life.

"Um, Jesse, I'd like the special."

Jesse's eyes narrowed. When he blinked, Lizzie halfway expected tattoos on the eyelids that said something like K-I-L-L or H-A-T-E.

"What special?" he said, looking at her like she was a bug.

Which was, of course, perfectly reasonable. Lizzie couldn't blame him. She was, after all, just a bug. Nothing more than a cockroach.

She swallowed hard. "The special, special." Her heart jackhammered.

"*You* want the special, special?" he asked, cocking his head in disbelief. "You?"

"It's for my boyfriend." Lizzie corrected herself. "My fiancée."

Jesse laughed, his entire body rolling with mirth. "Which one? And do your fiancée know about your boyfriend? You don't really seem the type."

Lizzie blinked. What was he saying?

Then she got it.

"Oh," she said. She forced a laugh. "Sorry. I just..."

Lizzie didn't know what to say, so she just let it hang there until she realized this Jesse might actually think she could actually do that, could actually have a fiancée and cheat on him with another man. But of course he did. Even this Jesse, a total stranger who'd known her for less than minute, could sense that she was a depraved woman who, at least if she were more beautiful, could have both a fiancée *and* a boyfriend.

She had no secrets from anyone.

"Oh my goodness, no," Lizzie said quickly. "They're the same. My boyfriend—" Her lips formed the letter P, and she almost blurted out his name, a slip Peter had warned her she better not do or face the most dire of consequences. But she just felt so flustered, her face suddenly feeling hot and sweat beading on her forehead. "I'd never do that."

Jesse snorted. "That's what they all say." He shrugged. "Although you, I probably believe it." He cocked his head again. "Tell me, if you engaged to be married, where's your diamond ring?"

Lizzie felt herself redden. It was back in the apartment, safe in her sock drawer. But could she say that? Could she admit out loud to this man that she hadn't been about to bring something so valuable down to Fuller Park? What would he think of that? It wasn't hard to guess.

She looked quickly all about her, spinning around, checking to make sure no one had snuck up on her and the fifteen hundred dollars that was most surely burning a hole in her pockets.

Jesse chuckled. "Let me guess. White girl like you ain't wearing no diamond ring cause you in Fuller Park. Think all we got here is muggers and thieves and worse. You take it off tonight for the first time since he give it to you. I bet you ain't never even been to Fuller Park before, am I right?"

Lizzie couldn't lie. She could only shake her head no.

"Could I, um, could I just please have the special, Mr., um, Mr. Jesse?" she asked, feeling as though a log had slid down her throat. Then a light went off in her head. "In fact, could I, um, could I get two of them? My boyfriend, I mean, my fiancée, seems"—and she suddenly realized she was talking far too much, just blabbing away, about to say that Peter seemed really afraid and nervous for the first time ever so this had to be really important, just blurting out what she almost certainly was supposed to keep secret—"um, if I could get two, that would be very much appreciated."

Jesse nodded. "Okay, two. But the special-special be a little more expensive tonight than usual. Gonna cost you."

Lizzie nodded rapidly. "Okay."

Jesse called over his shoulder. "A special-special for our special guest here. Two of them." He gave the eye to the tall girl running the fryer. She stood near six feet tall with broad shoulders. Almost certainly his daughter. Jesse turned back to Lizzie. "The special is a chimichanga. Beef or chicken?"

"No, I want the special-special," Lizzie said, confused. How could her intent have been misunderstood? No chimichanga on Earth could protect Peter. "Two special-specials."

Jesse leaned forward. "The special-special comes with the regular special, which tonight is a chimichanga. Beef. Or chicken."

"Oh," Lizzie said, then thought, *eeew!* Deep fried. How awful. Why not just inject the fat directly into the arteries? Although what did she expect at a taco truck, spinach salad and avocado toast?

"Could you make one of them vegetarian?"

Jesse roared with laughter. His tear tattoo danced. "You're getting the special-special—two of 'em—but you want your chimichanga vegetarian. That's a good one. Never got that before."

Lizzie waited. She was used to being laughed at.

Finally, Jesse settled down. "We don't do vegetarian. This is a fucking taco truck." He shook his head. "Excuse my language. Beef or chicken."

"I'm sorry." Lizzie stared down at the ground. "Beef, please, for both." She'd bring them both back to Peter, though they'd need to be reheated. She wasn't hungry.

"Seven each," Jesse said. "Fourteen total."

Ooof! Lizzie recoiled. That was a lot more than she had thought. She barely had enough. Good thing she brought extra. Peter had initially said a couple hundred for one. *Fourteen hundred dollars. Ouch!*

Lizzie couldn't remember ever having a funny thought before in her life. In fact, she didn't even understand what was funny about most jokes. They went right over her head. But a quip suddenly came to her and she blurted it out.

"These better be *really* good chimichangas."

Her eyes widened, and her hand flew to her mouth as if it could stuff the words back in.

But Jesse laughed. "Close to the best chimichangas we ever had."

Lizzie nodded and looked around. No one there. Out of her right pants pocket, she pulled the first seven hundred and fifty in wrapped twenties sandwiched inside a few tens, and palmed them over to Jesse, feeling like a spy. Then she pulled the identical roll out of her left pocket, removed the hundred in twenties she'd have left, and palmed the rest over to Jesse.

Jesse took the money in his huge hands, and it disappeared beneath the counter.

"I don't usually say this," he said, "but I see you do have a few dollars left. A tip never hurts. Could add an extra guarantee about the quality."

Lizzie wordlessly handed the extra hundred over. As long as she got out of here alive, and whatever she was purchasing kept Peter safe—*these better be really good chimichangas, had she really said that?*—then it was money well spent.

Minutes later, Jesse reappeared and handed her two large brown paper bags like the kind she got at the grocery store, but with the tops rolled up.

"See you next week," he said with a laugh.

Lizzie smiled weakly, her heart still in her throat, knowing he was having fun with her and not minding, just wanting to get back to her car and get out of here.

She locked the car doors as soon as she got in, and quickly drove off without looking at what was in the bags sitting on the passenger seat until she was well out of Fuller Park. The chimichangas smelled quite enticing, but she had no interest in food.

She finally stopped at a brightly lit, all-night Citgo station and convenience store. She didn't need gas. She'd topped the tank off earlier. But she pulled into the bay next to pump seven, well away from any other cars, and cautiously unrolled the top of one bag and opened it.

On top was the chimichanga wrapped in white paper

with a big smiley scribbled on top. Beneath it was a dirty white towel. Lizzie tugged at it.

Wrapped inside the towel was a gun and its magazine. She looked closer at the lettering on the slide. Glock 34Gen4 Austria 9x19.

Peter, what have you done?

THE INSTANT PETER saw the delicious babe in the slinky black, fuck-me dress walk into Flirts & Skirts, he knew he had to have her. He had a perfect view as she stood in the arched entranceway. His back was to the wall, the fifty-foot-long bar on his right running all the way to the rear, three deep with those waiting to order. The dance floor diagonally to his right was packed with patrons holding their drinks and moving to the pulsing music.

The smell of sex was in the air. Oh yeah. And Peter was a-sniffing. Perfume and cologne, too, and, of course alcohol. But mostly sex.

Peter sipped his Jack and Coke, felt the burn, and watched the delicious babe, clutching a small, black purse, avoid dancers and cut toward the bar. Going right across his field of view, only twenty feet away. It was no accident that he had a perfect view. He was no rookie.

Her hips swayed. Her tits jiggled. Long, jet-black hair flowed down her shoulders. Green eyes, perhaps, though it was hard to tell for sure in the club's scant light. Perfect makeup and long lashes.

Possibly a model, although here in Hyde Park she was

more likely another UC student. But holy shit, she could be a model. With just a touch of innocence.

Well, he'd take care of *that*. Oh yeah, he *had* to have this one.

One way or another.

And he *would* have her. Oh, yeah. Every which way but loose. And loose, too.

She was quite obviously alone. No boyfriend or concerned girlfriends to look after her, butting in. Peter smiled. It would be smooth sailing. She had come here to get nailed, and he was going to do the nailing.

Her legs flashed beneath her barely covered ass. Not just any legs. Spread-me-wide-and-pound-me-all-night-long legs. Make-me-walk-bowlegged-in-the-morning legs.

Oh yeah.

Peter moved to his right so their paths would intersect behind the three-deep throng waiting for drinks. When they collided, he turned to his left, saw her, and put a surprised look on his face.

"Sorry," he said, flashing his best smile. "Like sardines in here."

She eyed him warily, sized him up quickly, and clearly liked what she saw. Of course. He was wearing black jeans and a form-fitting dark blue shirt that showed off his physique. And he had great, soft hair that women loved. They all said so.

"Is this really the line to order a drink?" she asked.

"'Fraid so," Peter said. "I figured I'd get in line now with a half-full drink and it'll be gone by the time one of the bartenders gets to me."

"Tell me about it," she said.

"Hey, let me buy you a drink," Peter said, giving the beauty his most dazzling smile. "To make up for that Patrick Kane hip check I accidentally threw at you."

"Patrick who?"

"Patrick Kane. Black Hawks. I guess you're not a hockey fan, or not from here."

"Both."

Peter nodded. "Where you from?"

"Boston."

"Boo!"

Her perfectly trimmed eyebrows shot up. "Excuse me?"

"I've hated all the Boston sports teams since I was little. Hate 'em all."

Her eyes twinkled. "You hate us cause you ain't us."

"And here I thought I was falling in love with you."

She looked at him, sizing him up again, with eyes that were, in fact, green. He'd been right. "Slow down there, cowboy."

"Name's Peter."

"Alicia."

SHE WAS CAREFUL, this Alicia. Peter supposed all hot babes were—they had to be—and maybe plenty that weren't hot at all. They'd been warned about guys like him, so they were careful. Don't drink too much. Don't accept a drink from a stranger. Don't leave your drink unattended. Blah, blah, blah. Careful, careful, careful.

Fucking pains in the asses. But they almost always slipped up.

Alicia, too.

On her third Sex on the Beach, she eyed him carefully as he took the drink from the bartender and handed it to her, never taking her eye off it. But Peter hadn't studied magic for five years as a teenager for nothing. She never spotted the roofie he'd removed from his jeans pocket earlier, palmed, and then dropped in her drink as he passed it to her.

He even got fortunate after he took his own drink from the bartender and paid with a handsome tip. A bearded blond guy who had to be six-four and easily two-hundred-forty pounds—a fucking lumberjack dressed in a yellow-checked flannel shirt—bumped into Peter, and then asked if he could dance with Alicia.

"Fuck off!" Peter snapped.

"I believe it should be the lady's decision," the lumberjack said.

Peter glared. He was a good fighter. Had had lots of practice. But he didn't like his odds against this behemoth. "She's not interested." Peter almost added, but only thought, *why would she be interested in you when she can have me?*

Alicia touched his elbow, then spoke to the interloper. "I'm with Peter."

Only after the behemoth lumbered away did Peter realize the distraction had ensured the roofie had dissolved completely. It had been annoying to think the lumberjack was trying to take what was rightfully Peter's, but all's well that ends well.

Peter took a gulp of his Jack and Coke to calm his nerves and waited for Alicia to slip into oblivion. He thought of the many things he would do to her and smiled. Every which way but loose. And then loose, too.

And take photos, of course, for his ever-growing collection.

He hit the Jack and Coke again, then blinked. Alicia was looking at him funny. Or was it that she herself was looking funny?

Blurry?

Peter closed his eyes tightly, then opened them wide. Alicia was just a blur.

He blinked rapidly. The room with its pounding music spun faster and faster.

He tried to say, "What's happening?" but the words came out all jumbled up.

And then everything went black.

PETER AWOKE EARLY the next morning, lying naked in bed in a strange hotel room. The mother of all hangovers was crushing his skull. His stomach heaved and rolled like a ship pitching up and down on an angry sea. Sunlight streamed through the window, its shades wide open, piercing his eyeballs. His head was splintering apart, piece by piece into tiny sharp slivers. He was Humpty Dumpty, and they'd never put him back together again.

The room smelled of alcohol and sex. His mouth was cotton dry. Past the foot of the queen-sized bed, a TV sat on the right half of a wide laminated surface. Beneath it were empty storage cubes. To the left, a desk chair. The walls were painted with a bright orange shade that made Peter's already queasy stomach churn.

Where the fuck was he? As if in answer, Peter saw the navy-blue sign through the window.

MOTEL 6

WIFI HERE

Motel fucking 6? What the hell was he doing here? This wasn't the hotel he'd checked into last night before heading to Flirts & Skirts.

He rolled out of bed, and instantly regretted it, staggering on weak legs, almost falling flat on his face before realizing that he needed to get to the bathroom fast. He made it just in time, retching his guts out as he worshiped the porcelain god.

What the fuck.

With every bare-assed heaving of his guts, Peter's skull exploded and jagged flashes of lightning crossed his field of vision. *Kill me now.* When he could retch no more and even the dry heaves had mercifully stopped, he spit, grimacing at the sour taste in his mouth, and flushed the toilet for the sixth time.

He put his right arm across the back of the toilet seat and gently rested his Humpty Dumpty of a forehead on it. What the hell had happened?

The last thing he could remember was...

What?

Slowly it came to him. The tasty piece in the black fuck-me dress. What was her name? Couldn't remember.

But what difference did that make? He didn't give a flying fuck about any of their names. Other than as a label to go with the pictures.

Pictures. Yeah. Pictures. They'd jar his memory. If he couldn't remember the fun he'd had with... with... with whoever the fuck she was—

Alicia! That was it.

Had he brought her to this dump? Why, when he'd already checked in elsewhere, as usual getting a secluded room near the back? Well, she was gone now if she'd ever been here at all. And he couldn't remember a fucking thing. Which was a pity because she was quite the piece.

The pictures. They'd remind him. Where was the Nikon?

Peter staggered bare-assed back into the room toward the bed—painfully bright orange everywhere—and searched even as the room pitched and heaved around him.

The Nikon was nowhere to be found.

With growing alarm, Peter yanked the covers off the bed. Grabbed his boxers, jeans, and long-sleeved blue shirt off the floor. Tossed them onto the bed. Checked the storage cubes below the TV even though they were empty. Got down on all fours, almost collapsing in the process, and checked beneath the bed.

Searched every square inch.

Nothing.

The bitch had stolen the Nikon! And far more importantly, she had the memory card inside it that held his most prized possessions. Possessions that could not fall into the wrong hands. Peter's pulse pounded painfully in his brain.

Unless.

Unless he'd been so wasted—and he felt totally fucking trashed right now—that he hadn't even managed to get the Nikon out of the Acura's trunk. Had missed the opportunity to capture that bitch Alicia in all her glory. How totally wasted was that?

He sank to the bed and pulled on his clothes, not bothering with shoes and socks. Barefoot, he grabbed his keys and stepped out into the painful sunlight, wincing. Fortunately, the silver Acura ILX was parked directly in front of the first-floor room, less than ten feet away. He maybe couldn't do a hundred feet, but he could do ten. At least he'd followed that much of the usual plan. With his bare feet cold against first the concrete walkway and then the asphalt of the parking lot, Peter padded to the trunk, popped it with his key fob, and pulled back the carpet-and-cardboard cover atop the spare tire wheel well where he hid his Nikon SLR.

The black, hard-shell case was sitting right there where it was supposed to be. Relief and regret flooded over him simultaneously. Relief that the bitch hadn't stolen the camera and its priceless images after all. Regret that he hadn't captured any of her. How could he have missed an opportunity like that? She had to look glorious naked! And even better after that.

Wondering how he could possibly have been *that* wasted, Peter grabbed the case. His heart sank. It was far too light. He clicked open the latch.

The Nikon wasn't there. The case was empty.

Peter rocked back and forth on unsteady legs. The bitch *had* stolen it!

This couldn't be happening. Ninety-nine percent of the time, he kept it in its usual ultra-safe hiding place where not even the cops could find it. He brought it out only for nights like last night. So he could get the most perfect images possible. His iPhone, the latest model just recently released, was good, but it was no Nikon. And there were some memories that had to be captured in their most exquisite perfection.

But he couldn't afford for the Nikon to fall into the wrong hands. Its cost was the least of his worries. If nothing else, he could get Lizzie, who thought he was on a road trip with some friends to watch the UC football team play an away game, to buy him a new one. No, it was what was on the memory card that concerned him.

He rubbed his eyes, as if somehow that would magically make the Nikon reappear. It didn't. Peter stared at the empty case, then began to frantically search first his gym bag with its change of clothes, the rest of the trunk, and then all the car.

The Nikon was gone.

Mouth dry and still tasting of sour vomit, Peter licked his lips. He sank into the driver's seat, feet hanging out the open door. How could he have let this happen? He was always so careful, archiving the images on USB thumb drives that he encrypted and password protected before hiding. Even if uncovered by the police, they almost certainly couldn't crack his protection.

But thumb drives could go bad all by themselves. They could get ruined by fire or water damage. Or the PC he did the encryption on could fail, rendering the drives unreadable. None of that had happened to him, but he'd read about it.

And he just couldn't take the risk of ever losing those photos. Couldn't take the risk of losing those women. He *owned* them. So just in case, he'd kept the best photos on the Nikon, too, which wasn't as secure. Protecting images on a Nikon meant protecting them from accidental deletion, not from being able to view them on the camera itself.

And now it was in Alicia's hands. Possibly stolen this morning after he'd taken pictures of her last night. Peter ran his fingers through his hair. How could he have fucked up so badly? He'd have to call her and somehow get the camera back. Even if he had to beat it out of her. But he never exchanged numbers during hookups like this. Why make it easy to find him? And if she'd said her last name, he sure as shit couldn't remember it.

Just in case, Peter pulled his iPhone out of his jeans pocket. It had been a fucked up night. Maybe he had gotten her number. He thumbed the Home button.

He almost dropped the phone.

His head spun. Air rushed out of his lungs. He grabbed hold of the steering wheel to steady himself.

It couldn't be. This just wasn't possible.

But there it was in vivid color. His head propped up against a pillow. Inches away, two erect dicks, one white, one black, dangled over his wide-open mouth.

Peter gagged. He bent over and ducked his head outside the door. His empty stomach heaved. He retched uncontrollably over and over, dry heaving even as his head seemingly split in two.

There was no way he could ever have done that. Never, ever. There wasn't enough alcohol in the world to make him feel anything but total disgust for this.

He checked and saw there was just that one horrific photo. But, of course, one was all it took. *Other than that, Mrs. Lincoln, how did you like the play?*

How had someone unlocked his phone and taken that picture? That impossible, disgusting picture. Had he somehow been incapacitated and someone pressed his thumb to the Home button and unlocked the phone? How could—

Incapacitated.

Peter's panicked, fractured mind finally slipped the pieces into place. He figured out what should have been obvious to him soon after he woke up. He'd just been too wasted to see it.

That Alicia bitch had set him up. Set him up like a motherfucker.

She had roofied *him*!

PETER PICKED up his venti caramel macchiato with two extra shots of espresso and collapsed into a chair at a two-person table in the rear of the L-shaped Starbucks. The front tables along the floor-to-ceiling windows were mostly filled with customers noisily chatting and tapping away on laptops. Here in the rear, he was as far away from them as possible, his back turned to them, and he was shielded from the bright sunlight streaming in.

He set the drink down on the circular light-brown tabletop, took off the cup's cover to let the steaming-hot liquid cool, and rubbed his eyes. On another day, he'd enjoy the smell of the steamed milk and espresso along with the vanilla syrup.

Not today.

At the Motel 6, he'd taken a long, hot shower, and changed into the clean clothes he'd packed for the fictitious UC football team road trip: jeans and a long-sleeved, pullover Bears T-shirt of navy blue and burnt orange. But he still felt like shit. He still couldn't believe what his eyes had told him. What his lying eyes had told him.

Now, he needed to think. Even if his brain wasn't cooperating. What the fuck had actually happened? And what the hell was he going to do about it?

He blew on the drink and ventured a sip, getting more caramel drizzle than coffee. It was still too hot, but he needed the caffeine so he took another small sip. Did it really matter at this point if he burned his mouth to a fucking crisp?

"Hey, buddy, how's it hanging?"

The blond, bearded lumberjack from last night slapped Peter on the back and sat down, dropping two large manila envelopes on the table. They landed heavily with an ominous, loud thwack. The huge lumberjack again wore a checked flannel shirt, its golden yellow matching his hair and beard.

"Who the fuck are you?" Peter asked. "What are you doing here?"

The lumberjack leaned close, his thick forearms on the table, and grinned. "I'm your worst fucking nightmare."

A few pieces to the sickening puzzle clicked into place, but not all of them. The lumberjack, who had to be at least six-four, and two-hundred-forty, rock-hard pounds, had been at Flirts & Skirts, trying to hone in on Alicia. So how did he fit in?

Peter put the cover back onto the cup and sipped the still-too-hot macchiato, burning his mouth but not showing it, projecting only nonchalance. He had to stay cool. Never let the other asshole even *think* he's getting the upper hand. Even if you've got the equivalent of seven-deuce off-suit, act like you've got aces. But his heart raced.

Peter took another sip. His eyes bored in on the blond lumberjack's cold blue eyes. Again, Peter asked, "Who the fuck are you?"

"You can call me Sven," the lumberjack said. "That's not my real name. Any more than Alicia is my partner's real name. But close enough."

Partner? The word punched Peter in the gut. Things were as bad as he'd feared. Worse. He sank back in his seat, suddenly nauseous. *Your worst fucking nightmare.*

"Partners?" Peter finally managed to ask. "You're like, a couple?"

Sven, the lumberjack, shook his head. "Purely business."

"What do you want?"

Sven smiled. "Everything."

"What do you mean?"

He tapped the two manila envelopes. "We own you, motherfucker."

Peter tried to calm his racing heart and clear the thoughts clanging about inside his brain like a pinball. He'd known his life had turned to pure hell as soon as he'd seen the empty Nikon case and the picture on his phone hours ago, but it was a far hotter hell than he'd imagined.

Steadying his trembling hands, Peter spread his arms wide. "Whatever you think you got on me, I don't have any money."

Sven gave Peter a shooing-away motion.

"You rich boys always cry poor," Sven said. "But you live in a nice apartment, you drive a fancy car, you're wearing designer jeans and Nikes, which each cost a couple hundred dollars, and you're here drinking a six-dollar cup of coffee. Spare me the bullshit. You got money coming out of your ass."

"Honest to God, I'm broke," Peter said. "It's my bitch that has the money. She pays for everything. The apartment. The car. The clothes. Everything." He stopped himself before he added that Lizzie had even paid for her own engagement ring. No need for this prick to know about *that*. "She even puts money on my Starbucks card. That's how I paid for this six-dollar coffee, which thanks to you now tastes like shit."

"Sounds like she's your meal ticket."

"You could say that," Peter said. "But I can't exactly

ask her to pay for this… this thing you think you have on me."

"Then I guess you better not let her find out what you've been doing." Again, Sven tapped the envelopes. "Otherwise, your meal ticket goes bye-bye. In fact, she might be the first person we send high-res copies of the photos so she can see every last detail. Before, of course, we paper the walls of UC with them." He slid the top envelope to Peter. "Check it out."

Peter froze.

Sven reached over and slipped the top two photographs out of the envelope. One showed Peter lying on his back. The other showed him on all fours. In both he was naked. Both with two men, one white, one black.

"Got a couple hundred different shots in here," Sven said. "Want to see them?"

The room spun. Peter felt himself about to black out.

"Put those away," he somehow managed to say. "Put them away!"

Sven slid them back in the envelope.

Peter gripped the table to steady himself.

"That isn't me! I'm not—!" He couldn't even say the word. "Not even close!"

"These pictures would argue otherwise. And the one on your phone."

"But I'm not! Never once! That shit disgusts me. I don't know what you did, but that isn't me. You doctored those photos! I would never—"

"Oh, you were quite cooperative," Sven said, beaming. "We didn't have to use your thumbprint to unlock your phone. You were quite happy to tell us your password. All your passwords. Where your car was parked in the Flirts & Skirts parking lot. You handed the keys right over. Oh, you were quite chatty with Alicia. Though not so much with the two guys."

Peter felt his face grow hot and his stomach wretch.

"They didn't really do anything to me, did they?" he said, trying to keep the begging out of his voice. "It was all just staged. Faked. Right?"

Sven shrugged. "I don't know. You tell me. How's your asshole feel?"

Peter lunged across the table but stopped himself halfway. He wanted to rip the guy's heart out of his chest and devour the bloody organ, bite by bite, bit by bit. He wanted to kill the motherfucker. Rip his goddamned smiling face off. Tear that blond beard out by the roots. Wanted to make him suffer.

But not only could the lumberjack tear him in two, the piece of shit also had him by the balls.

Peter sank back in his chair, suddenly short of breath. He looked over his shoulder. No one from the front of Starbucks had noticed.

"Good for you that you didn't touch me," Sven said. "That would have driven up the price. A lot."

"I got no money. What do you want me to do?"

"Then you'll work it off."

"What does that mean?"

"If all else fails, you're a nice piece of ass." Sven smiled grimly. An icy hardness filled his eyes. "And I'm not talking servicing the cougars of Chicago. Your photos from last night could be advertisements. Young, supple flesh. Submissive. We could sell you to enterprises that specialize in that sort of thing."

Peter thought he might vomit all over the table. There wasn't much left in his stomach to puke up, but it was still a struggle to hold down whatever was there. He tried to calm his heaving gut. Clenched his eyes. Sucked in a deep breath. Listened to the jackhammering of his heart and tried to slow the beat.

Slowly. Slowly. Slowly.

Finally, he opened his eyes. The nightmare was still sitting across from him, of course, huge arms crossed, looking down on him as if he were just a bug.

"You've ruined my life!" Peter said through clenched teeth. "Why? Why me?"

"I think you know."

"No, I don't! Why couldn't you have picked some... some *bisexual* freak who wouldn't care. Why me?" Peter shuddered.

"It's about giving you what you deserve, Peter."

Peter recoiled at the familiar use of his name. Of course, the man knew his identity. He'd been through his wallet. He'd...he'd....Peter tried to push it all from his mind but couldn't.

You tell me. How's your asshole feel?

Please God, Peter thought, let it all have been staged. I'll go to Mass every Sunday for the rest of my life if it was just staged. They couldn't possibly have really...really....

He squirmed in his seat, not really sure how his asshole felt.

"Why me?" he asked again.

"Alicia selected you," Sven said. "She always picks the

target. She's good at it. She seems to know which guys are going to try to do what you tried. She has an instinct for that sort of thing. Lots of experience, I guess. Plus in your case, it was easy. A while back, you tried something on a friend of a friend of a friend."

"What do you mean?"

"Don't play dumb. We know."

"I was just—"

"We've got your Nikon. We know." Sven slid the top manila envelope aside and tapped the bottom one. "I could show you these photos, but they won't shock you at all. You already know them by heart. In fact, they really make our photos irrelevant. These are much better for our purposes."

Peter's life, already pushed off a cliff and plummeting to the jagged rocks far below, crash-landed, exploding into bits of dust.

"You were going to do to Alicia the same thing you did to all those girls on the camera," Sven said. "Roofie her. Take her to a remote room at the back of some motor lodge, carry her inside, and take your pictures. Of you pulling her clothes off. Then raping her as she lay there helpless, either unconscious or incoherent. Incapacitated one way or another. No other word for it. Rape."

Peter looked over his shoulder to make sure no one had gotten close enough to hear.

"I don't know what you're talking about," he said, unable to come up with anything more original than that oldest, lamest line in the book. "I don't even own a Nikon."

Sven smiled. "Not anymore."

All the air went out of Peter's lungs.

"If the police get those pictures," Sven said, "you'll be taking it up the ass in jail from guys even bigger than me. Hard, hard time. Especially for a cute guy like you." Sven nodded. "Real hard time, motherfucker."

Peter couldn't speak for what felt like an eternity. And Sven sat there smugly, letting it all sink in.

"How did Alicia do it?" Peter finally asked, although he thought he'd figured it out.

"She caught you spiking her drink," Sven said, his blue eyes cold and merciless. "We only do this to scumbags like you. We have no innocent victims. Only scumbags who deserve what's coming to them."

"But I didn't—"

Sven cut him off with a wave of his thick hand.

"You were pretty good palming the roofie, but nothing gets past Alicia. Not anymore. You'd have to be Penn and fucking Teller to fool Alicia. So she gave me the eye. Set the wheels in motion. I distracted you so she could drop a roofie in *your* drink. Lights out, Chicago."

"That fucking bitch!" Peter muttered.

"Nah, you know what's the bitch? Payback is the fucking bitch."

Peter glanced over his shoulder to again make sure no one was listening. "So this is like some fucking crusade for you two?"

"It is for Alicia," Sven said. "It's a holy war she's been fighting ever since a piece of shit succeeded doing to her what you just tried. She was a bit naïve back then. Not anymore. So she'd do this for free. Just for the street justice. But me? It ain't no holy war for me. Just a business. Sure beats working for a living. And the pay is *phenomenal.*"

"Let me talk to Alicia," Peter said, taking the longest of long shots. He'd always been able to sweet-talk women. "I could explain."

"How are you going to explain?" Sven asked, shaking his head in disbelief. "With most of the rapist-wannabes, we just have them spiking her drink, and that's all she needs. But with you, we've got the camera, too. Pictures of you assaulting all those girls you roofied. You're not just a wannabe; you've succeeded over and over. We got you red-handed. Not even the ghost of Johnnie Cochran could get you acquitted with Alicia.

"Besides, she's out of the picture now. She doesn't like this part of the business. Gets a little squeamish at the dirty stuff. Doesn't want to know anything about it. Like they say about sausage. She doesn't want to know how the messy sausage of justice is made. She only wants to eat it. And we sure as shit are gonna make sausage out of you." Sven smiled wolfishly. "Alicia just takes her cut and lets the knowledge of getting some street justice try to heal that broken part of her soul. Least that's what she says. '*That broken part of my soul.*' Kinda poetic, I think. Don't you?"

Peter said nothing.

"So you'll never see her again," Sven said. "Unless, of course, you see her at another club sometime, hunting for predators like you. But probably not. We move around. As you might guess, we've got a few enemies. Can't stay in any one place for long."

Beneath the table, Peter clenched and unclenched his

fists. His balls were in a vice and the fucking lumberjack was turning the crank. Enjoying himself. Knowing he didn't want to hear the answer, Peter asked the million-dollar question.

"How much are we talking about?"

He almost fell off his chair when he heard it.

"Five thousand for most guys, but not for you. We're not talking about just the embarrassment some creep feels about pictures like these getting out or getting into the hands of a wife. We're talking felonies. Lifetime in prison without parole felonies. The Nikon changes everything."

"How much?"

"For you, a hundred thousand for everything. You get all the photos, the originals, and the Nikon."

Peter's jaw dropped. "You can't be serious!" He didn't bother to ask how there could be any guarantee that copies hadn't already been made for future blackmailing purposes. He was no fool. They most certainly had. That didn't matter.

A hundred thousand!

"I'd be lucky if I could pay a grand."

"We do have an installment plan," Sven said, smiling.

Peter just stared, struggling to comprehend all of what he'd just heard.

His life was over.

Sven slid the top manila envelope to him. The one with the sickening pictures of him and the two men. "Take these. We don't need them." He tapped the other envelope. "This is all that matters now."

Peter pushed the envelope back. He didn't even want to touch it. "I don't want these."

"Fine," Sven said. "I'll leave them out front on a table by the cash register."

Peter grabbed the envelope back even as it made his skin crawl. "You fucking asshole! Both of you!"

Sven took a phone out of his pants pocket and slid it to Peter. A burner.

"Use this to text or call me. Only me, no one else. My number is in there. Don't say words like 'money' or 'photographs' or the always popular, 'you fucking cocksucker.' You never know who's listening. Use code names like 'delivery' and 'package'. If you don't contact me in forty-eight hours to arrange at least a down payment of five thousand dollars, I'll send your Nikon and this second envelope to the police and tell them where to find you. I can only imagine the price of your bail."

"I can't pay," Peter said.

"Then next time we meet, give yourself an enema first. Clean yourself out. And bring plenty of lube."

———

THE SMELL of the chimichangas filled the Hyundai, but Lizzie wasn't even tempted. All she could do as she sat parked beneath the brightly lit canopy of the Citgo station was stare at the two paper bags. Stare and wonder, *Peter, what have you done?*

She'd peeked in the second bag, too, and its contents were identical to the first. A chimichanga wrapped in white paper with a smiley on top, no longer hot but not yet cold, and beneath it, the same model Glock and its magazine wrapped inside a dirty white towel.

She couldn't imagine what trouble Peter was in to need a gun. And not just any gun. A gun secretly purchased with cash slipped furtively to a guy in, of all places, a taco truck, and dispensed in a brown paper bag tucked beneath a chimichanga.

An untraceable gun. A bootleg gun that could be used and gotten rid of, even if two of them cost *fourteen hundred dollars* (plus tip). Gotten rid of because it had been used in a crime. If not murder, then at least threatening it.

Peter, what have you done? What are you planning to do?

His words came back to her. *It's better that you don't know.* He was probably right about that. But she let that same logic guide her own decision about the second gun. It might be best if Peter didn't know she had it. She couldn't imagine actually committing a crime (other than buying an illegal gun, of course). But she could watch out for him. Be his backup—the one nobody saw coming—and make sure nothing went wrong.

Of course, something was about to go wrong and she knew it. But what could Peter do with a second gun? Firing two guns a-blazing was something that happened only in old Westerns. Better that she be able to ride to his rescue, or at least try to, if things did run amuck.

She would be his insurance policy.

She could handle a gun. Her father had taken her to a shooting range several times when she was sixteen after their house had been broken into. But she hadn't liked it.

Especially after she found herself pretending the target was Uncle Bob. And then her mother. And finally herself.

Ooof!

Lizzie shook herself like a dog coming out of water. She'd made her decision and that was that. She wouldn't tell Peter because, in his own words, *it's better you don't know*. He'd probably get it out of her. He'd even gotten her to tell him about Julie. When it came to loose lips sinking ships, her ship might as well be already at the bottom of the ocean.

But she could at least try. She'd protect her future husband, no matter who was threatening him.

Lizzie rolled the nearest bag up tight, got out of the car, and put the bag in the trunk in the spare wheel well, then covered it with a pile of blankets.

She would stand by her man.

WHERE IS SHE? Where is that stupid bitch? Peter paced back and forth inside the apartment. *How long does it take to drive to Fuller Park and back?*

The fleeting thought occurred to him that Lizzie might have gotten hurt or killed or at least robbed. If so, he was fucked. He had no contingency plan for a gun beyond the taco truck. He was counting on the silly twit, God help him.

Peter froze when the key turned in the lock, then he all but tackled her when Lizzie stepped inside the apartment. She started to take off her coat and say something, but he had no time for that shit.

"Let me see it," Peter said, snatching the bag from Lizzie's hand and taking a peek inside. He fumbled past the wrapping of some warm tortilla-like thing, then felt the reassuring outline of a pistol inside the towel. *Yes!* He wanted to take it out and examine every microscopic detail, touch the cold metal, and smell the gun oil. But there was business to take care of first. He narrowed his eyes. "Did you look inside? Don't lie to me!"

Lizzie went all doe-eyed and meek. "You never said I couldn't."

"I must have! And if I didn't, I shouldn't have had to! For fuck's sake, you're a 4.0 in pre-med. Do I have to spell everything out for you?"

"Peter, all you said was to take a thousand dollars into Fuller Park and find a taco truck. I did what you said."

"Are you giving me an attitude?"

"No."

"You better not or you'll be taking your exams next week standing up!"

Lizzie just blinked.

"I'm serious!" he said, then remembered he needed her to pony up more cash. To make the setup look legit. "Hey, I'm sorry." He stroked her cheek. "I'm obviously under a lot of stress." He forced a smile. "Well, since you've already stuck your nose into it"—he shook his head—"let's take a look."

He slid the contents of the bag onto the kitchen table, tossed the wrapper with the tortilla or whatever the fuck it was at the sink and missed—it hung on the edge of the counter—and unwrapped the gun.

"*Oooh!*" Peter said, a warm sensation filling his gut as

he slid the web of his hand into the grip and touched his finger to the trigger. "A Glock 34 Gen 4. *Nice!* And in mint condition." He popped the magazine in, popped it out, racked the slide, then popped the magazine back in. He eyed the gun from end to end, holding it up under the ceiling light to see it better. "I was afraid I might get something last used by Wild Bill Hickok. You never know with a place like that."

"Peter, what's happened to you? What's wrong?" Lizzie asked, the sound of her pleading voice taking the edge off the thrill of holding the gun.

"Like I told you before," Peter said between clenched teeth, "it's best you don't know. What you don't know can't hurt you. That's why I didn't want you to open the fucking bag." He waved the Glock. "Didn't want you to see this."

Peter wondered if by some miracle his entire plan did work, would he have to kill Lizzie to leave no loose ends behind? It would tidy things up for sure, but the cops always looked for the boyfriend first. Always. So he could forget that idea. Besides, controlling Lizzie was *never* a problem. If he couldn't keep her silly yap shut, he'd point the gun at his own head and pull the trigger.

"I'm scared," Lizzie said. "I was scared to death in Fuller Park! But even more, I'm scared for you. For whatever must be happening to you. I love you! I want to help."

"Yeah, yeah. I bet it was scary," Peter said, nodding. "Hey, how much is left of the thousand?"

Lizzie looked like she was going to cry. "Nothing."

"*Nothing?* There's nothing left?"

Lizzie shook her head, wide-eyed.

"That bastard charged you a grand?" Peter shook his head, then reconsidered. The Glock 34 Gen 4 was a fine piece of machinery. Most importantly, there was no paper trail. Plus, it was just Lizzie's money. What did he care? But shit, a thousand?

"Listen, I'm going to need another grand," he said. "How soon can you get it?"

"*Another* thousand dollars?" Lizzie cried. "Peter, I've got almost no more money left."

He wanted to slap her. But he counted to three. Once, twice, and then a third time. He took a deep breath. If he made it out of all of this alive, the bitch would be in for more pain than she ever imagined.

"I can't explain it to you," he said in as even a tone as he could manage. "It wouldn't be safe. But I only need the money for an hour and then I'll give it back. I need it for show. I hate to deplete your *fucking* bank account, but this is to save my life."

Lizzie nodded eagerly. "Of course."

"And I'm going to need to use your car. I'm not sure the time yet, but probably nine o'clock or later. A nice car like the Acura is too memorable." He smiled, trying to be charming, though he doubted that he needed to bother. "Your bucket-of-bolts old Hyundai is just what I need."

"Okay."

"Now go get some sleep and forget everything you've seen or heard the last few hours. They didn't happen. Got that? Never happened."

Lizzie nodded so eagerly she looked like a fucking bobblehead doll.

"If I'm not here for dinner, leave the money and your car keys under my pillow. Make sure they're there no later than six o'clock. Then clear out. Go to the library or somewhere. I don't want to see you."

Lizzie put her hand up timidly, like a fucking fifth-grader asking the teacher to speak.

"What?" Peter snapped.

"Can't I do anything to help?"

"You can help me by getting the fucking money and then getting out of the fucking way. I don't want you distracting me. And it's best you don't see a fucking thing. Understood?"

WITH THE SNIVELING bitch out of the way and soon snoring loudly—if only he could get away with taking a pillow, clamping it down hard over her fucking mouth, and silencing her forever!—Peter closed the bedroom door and moved to the picture window overlooking the street. Below there was only darkness, broken by the orange glow of streetlamps and the headlights of the occasional car.

It was now past two in the morning. Probably too late to call or text the asshole, but he might still be up.

Peter typed into the burner, *We need to talk.*

The phone rang. Peter answered.

"Do you realize what time it is?" Sven asked.

"Am I interrupting your beauty sleep?"

"Not at all. I'd just think you wouldn't want to piss me off."

"Like you could make things any worse for me?"

Sven snickered. "Don't tempt me."

"We need to talk."

"We're talking."

"In person."

"Not happening. Either you make your delivery or I make mine."

"I can't do it, but I've got an offer you might be interested in."

"You seem to think I'm willing to negotiate."

"I can make a partial delivery and make up for the shortfall."

"How?"

"We need to meet in person. Even burners can be eavesdropped on. And I need to show you my offer. Make my presentation. Plus, of course, make the partial delivery."

"How much of a partial delivery?"

"One. I know it ain't five, but it's a good-faith partial. And you'll be interested in what I've got to show you. I guarantee it."

Sven went silent. Peter held his breath. This was just one of the many pieces that had to come together to even give him a chance. He had to be right about all his guesses, and a lot of luck had to go his way. Even then, he'd still be a long shot to come out of it alive. But if this first piece to the puzzle didn't happen, he didn't have a chance.

"When?" Sven finally said.

"I'm getting the partial during the day tomorrow. So anytime tomorrow night. You pick the time and place."

"Nine o'clock. Get in your car then and start driving. I'll call you and tell you where to go."

LIZZIE HATCHED the plan in her free hour between Biochemistry and Cell Biology. It took her seventeen minutes because it wasn't a good plan. It was preposterous to think it could somehow work—it only put her in a position to help Peter, nothing more—and almost everything could go wrong. But it was the best she could do.

The idea came to her during the first of the seventeen minutes because, of course, it was obvious considering where she'd left the Glock. *Her* Glock, as she now thought of it. Sixteen minutes later, she hadn't thought of anything else. Creativity was not her strong suit. In truth, it wasn't a suit at all. She would have kept trying—she would try forever for Peter—but she theorized that perhaps her subconscious could do better so she switched to her studies for the other forty-three minutes. But even her subconscious came up empty.

So after leaving her car keys and the money under the pillow as commanded—this thousand dollars had required a cash advance on her MasterCard because the checking account had truly been sucked dry—Lizzie slipped outside to her Hyundai, which she'd left unlocked minutes before. She popped the trunk, locked the doors, and after checking to make sure that no one was watching, climbed into the trunk, legs on the driver's side, and pulled it shut. Shifting to lay on her left side, she snuggled beneath the three thick woolen blankets she'd brought down earlier along with a warm coat, just in case, and hunkered down in the darkness for what might be a long wait.

She'd done her homework. Lizzie Hosker always did her homework. These were cramped quarters, to be sure, no matter how tiny she was. Her knees were bent so they came halfway up to her chest. But she'd manage. She certainly wasn't claustrophobic, not after the various hoods and other paraphernalia that Peter employed. And there was no danger of becoming locked in the trunk. The Hyundai, as did all cars since the turn of the century, came with an internal trunk release that required a mere flick of a glowing orange knob to open it. The trunk was far from air-tight. She wouldn't suffocate. The blankets and coat would keep her warm even if the late-night air turned cold. She'd drank no liquids since this morning, and she'd peed just before she came down.

Beneath the covers were the three things she thought needed: a tiny flashlight no larger than a AA battery, her phone set to silent mode, and the Glock. As prepared as possible.

In the end, though, she wasn't prepared at all.

PETER HAD BEEN DRIVING the Hyundai in random directions, cursing with every right and left he took, for twenty minutes before he got the call on the burner. He'd hidden the Glock in the underside of the dashboard, duct-taping it with just a single thin strip to the back of the paneling where the paneling ended and the steering column extended to the front end assembly. His tiny bottle of pepper spray, so small he could palm it undetected, was nestled in a "magician's" sleeve sewn into the underside of his shirt at the right elbow.

He knew he was a prohibitive long shot. His guesses needed to be correct, and plenty of luck had to fall his way. Even with all that, he'd still probably fail.

But he was going down with all guns blazing. Fucking Lizzie and her kind would just roll over and take it, but not him. No way was he going to jail. No way was he going to pay a blackmailer, especially since copies had been made of everything. He'd be forever under the thumb of that shithead Sven, powerless to wriggle free. Peter wasn't about to pay forever in cash or services of any kind, whether it be selling his ass—no fucking way! —or muling drugs or anything.

If he could actually cash in a life insurance policy on himself, he'd buy a big one right now because a long life culminating in a quiet retirement was not in the cards. Odds had to be a million-to-one against him being alive a year from now. Hell, a month from now. For fuck's sake, maybe even a day from now. He was holding a shitty hand and Sven held aces. But Peter was ready to crack those aces into tiny little pieces. And if he didn't? Better a bullet in the head than a dick up his ass. Even a metaphorical one.

So when Sven's circuitous directions led Peter to a deserted street in a rundown area with boarded-up triple-decker houses on the right and a football-field-sized vacant lot on the left, he pulled to the curb alongside the triple-deckers, well aware that his body might soon be lying in the lot across the street. But with a shit-ton of luck, the body would instead be Sven's.

"Pull underneath the streetlamp, turn on the interior overhead light, and turn off the car," Sven dictated over the burner phone. "Put the cash on the passenger seat next to you. Then put your hands in the air and touch the ceiling."

Peter followed the orders even though no other car, and no other person, was in sight.

"No sudden movements or you're a dead man," Sven said. "Put the phone on speaker, roll down the window, and put the phone on the roof."

Peter did as instructed.

"Slowly, and I mean slowly or it'll be the last fucking thing you do," came the command over the speaker phone from the roof, "slowly reach through the window, use the handle to open the door, and with your hands up, slowly get out."

Peter grimly did so. *Good-bye Glock.*

"Hands against the hood. Spread your legs."

Peter complied, even as the cold air rippled through his shirt and chilled his skin.

A black SUV skidded to a stop behind the Hyundai, high beams supplemented by blinding floodlights. Car doors opened.

Peter's heart sank even further. Two car doors had opened, one right after another. It had been a long shot, but he had hoped he would be going up against Sven *mano a mano*. The huge blond had approached him alone in Starbucks and had then talked almost exclusively about him and Alicia. He'd then said that Alicia got squeamish at the dirty side of the business, so she left that to him. She wanted to eat the sausage without knowing how it was made.

Eat my sausage, you fucking bitch! Peter thought, then tried to calm back down. He had to think straight. Be cool.

So no Alicia. Sven had also made it seem as though it was just a two-person operation, him and Alicia. Whoever the two men were who had at least pretended to rape him in the pictures—had they actually... penetrated him? Peter wasn't sure he wanted to know—it sounded like they were just a couple of fucking perverts who did what they did for free. For the fucking fun of it. Or else they were hired hands, locals that didn't travel with Sven and Alicia as they crisscrossed the country in their campaign of harsh street justice. An especially likely possibility if his "scenes" had just been staged, and not the real thing. Just local actors with a sick fucking sense of humor.

But Peter knew now his assumption—or had it been wishful thinking?—that he was only against the two ring-leaders, one of whom didn't like the dirty stuff, was false.

Someone else was back there with Sven. Maybe one of the actors—please God, Peter hoped, let them be actors and not perverts—but maybe this was an even larger operation and the extra was a bodyguard. Or a hit man.

So much for having even a long shot of a chance.

Footfalls crunched briefly on the potholed asphalt, sounding like one from each side of the SUV, then stopped, maintaining a safe distance out of range of the pepper spray. If Peter could even get at it without getting shot first.

Peter glanced back, but blinded by the harsh floodlights mounted atop the SUV, he could only make out two vague shapes dressed all in black, including black ski masks covering their faces. Sven's huge shape from the driver's side and a short guy on the other. Just the two vague shapes and the glint of steel. Pistols.

"Hands up!" yelled Sven from the driver's side. "Turn and face the front of your car! Your back to me!"

Peter had hoped that the smug, cavalier prick who'd approached him alone in Starbucks would be arrogant enough—or shorthanded enough if the perverts weren't really part of the picture—to either make some kind of mistake or give Peter some opening. But the prick wasn't alone and he hadn't made a single mistake.

"What the fuck is up with the change of cars?" Sven demanded. "Where's the Acura? I ought to shoot you right now!"

"Relax," Peter said. "It's an old piece of shit. I figured you're probably gonna kill me anyway no matter what I do. Why ruin a nice car if you're going to fill it with bullet holes?"

"You trying to be a wise guy?"

"No, I just like that Acura. And thought it might catch attention. It's a nice car. I didn't know you'd be bringing me someplace like this."

"Try anything funny and it's your fucking funeral."

"I got it. I ain't gonna try anything funny."

Silence hung in the air for a long time. Peter

wondered if Sven and his accomplice were sending each other hand signals or something.

"Cash is on the passenger seat?" Sven finally asked.

"Yes."

"Okay, turn your back to the cash. Face the other side of the street. Face the vacant lot you're gonna get buried in if you try anything funny."

Gravel crunched, then behind Peter, the Hyundai's passenger door opened. A rustling sound came from the seat, presumably the cash being stuffed in a bag.

"So what's your business proposal?" Sven asked.

"Can I put my hands down?" Peter asked, his right hip against the open door, still blinded by the radiant floodlight.

"No!"

Sven, still masked, remained twenty feet away, his pistol trained on Peter. The short guy was presumably on the other side of the Hyundai, his sights aimed at the back of Peter's head.

Two guns vs. none. *Say good-night, Peter boy.*

Other than the last card he still had left to play, his pathetic excuse for a proposal had boiled down to "lure you here with a thousand bucks, then try to get you to make a mistake." A piece-of-shit plan, to be sure, one that Sven had shredded to pieces, but it wasn't as though Peter had been able to enlist Little Miss Four-point-fucking-oh to come up with anything better. The bitch was useless for anything like this. Useless for almost anything except this last card.

A wild card. Time to play it.

"The woman I live with," Peter said, "I've bled her dry.

She said there's nothing left and I believe her. And like I told you before, I ain't got any money myself. Now you can talk all you want about selling my ass on the streets, but I hate queers. I'll either kill someone or kill myself. I'm not a valuable commodity.

"But the woman is another story. She'll take it. She's been taking it all her life. She'll take it forever. You, or someone you sell her to, can make a mint off her if you do it right. She can be a fucking gold mine.

"She's no beauty. Kind of a Plain Jane type. Tiny, barely five feet tall. Almost no tits at all. But you can use that to your advantage. A while back I got her to shave her pussy. She looks like she's only twelve years old.

"Put her in pigtails and a Catholic schoolgirl dress, and she'll be the dream of every kiddie fiddler in Chicago. Detroit. New York City. Wherever. And she takes a whipping. Oh yeah, she can take a hellacious whipping. I can show you pictures and everything. Got 'em on my phone right here.

"So let's deal. My ass for hers. She's got no living family. No friends at all. I'm all she's got. I'll cover with the school. I'll come up with something, and no one will even know that she's gone. Ain't no one will give a shit. Trust me. Let me show you the pictures! I got 'em right here."

<hr>

WHEN THE CAR had started moving, Lizzie's heart skipped a beat. Finally! She wasn't sure if it was a good thing or a bad thing, but they were moving. The rubber smell of the spare tire filled the trunk's cold, close air. Lizzie listened in vain for Peter's voice—she needed to hear his voice!—as she lay there beneath the blankets, legs cramping, eyes wide, her hands inches from the gun. They seemed to be driving around in what seemed like aimless fashion, making the same uncomfortable turns one after another.

Then the phone rang and she heard Peter's reassuring voice. At first just specifying what street they were on, and then a lot of "okay" and "yes" reactions to commands she couldn't hear.

But it was good to hear his voice. Lizzie exhaled in relief. Her racing heart calmed ever so slightly.

Until the car stopped.

Lizzie sucked in a gulp of air. Her hand gripped the Glock. Her heart jackhammered. Then he began to talk about her.

"The woman I live with, I've bled her dry," Peter said.

No, Peter!

But it got worse. So much worse.

As he continued on, she had all she could do not to cry out in pain. A pain far worse than all his most extreme punishments.

Her heart broke into tiny little shards.

When he completed his proposal—" My ass for hers…. Ain't no one will give a shit"—Lizzie's heart ceased to exist.

"THAT'S NOT a proposal Alicia will go for," Sven said with what sounded to Peter like an odd, almost comical tone in his voice. "You know she's in this gig because of what happened to her. So when you tried to roofie her, she had no sympathy for you. How's she going to okay a trade of you, someone who was going to rape her, for the innocent woman you live with?"

"Fuck Alicia!" Peter said, gaining hope that he might actually be getting through to Sven, actually had a chance. He might pull the rabbit out of the hat after all. "Alicia doesn't have to know. This can be your deal. Just between you and me. Cut in Shorty, the guy behind me, if you want, or keep all the money yourself. Fuck her and the horse she rode in on."

"Hey, asshole," came a female voice from the other side of the car. "I'm not into horses."

It took a moment for the voice to register. And then...

Aw, fuck. It was Alicia.

Peter closed his eyes and took a deep breath. Resigned, he said to Sven, "I thought you said she doesn't like the dirty work." He gestured over his shoulder toward Alicia. "What the hell is she doing here?"

"I'm making an exception for you, you asshole," Alicia said. "I'm making an exception for a guy who likes raping incapacitated women so much he has to take photos as mementos of the cherished events. Those photos are going to land you in jail, motherfucker, because this thousand dollars is all we're gonna take from you. 'Cause your Nikon is going to the cops as soon as we leave here so you can rot in jail for the rest of your miserable fucking existence."

LIZZIE LAY in the trunk unable to move. She had gone from hurt to crushed to...

Destroyed.

This was the man she was going to marry? This monster? Had he ever loved her? Of course, he hadn't. She was unlovable. No wonder he... no wonder he...

She had to ask him if he had *ever* cared for her at all.

Lizzie hit the glowing orange knob. The trunk hood popped up.

PETER HEARD a noise from the back of the car and didn't think twice. He wasn't going to get a better opportunity.

He dove onto the front seat, legs dangling out the door, and reached for the Glock strapped to the back of the underpanel. In his peripheral vision, he saw Alicia, off to the right and no longer wearing a ski mask, swing her gun to face the rear of the car.

From behind on his side, a shot boomed.

Peter's knee exploded. Pain tore through him. He screamed. Streaks flashed across his eyes. *Motherfucker!*

But primal instinct kept him moving. Peter tore the gun free from the underpanel. Racking the slide, he rolled onto his back. Sat half-up.

The trunk had somehow popped up, leaving only a small opening in the top right corner of the rear window where he could see Sven's huge frame.

Peter fired. The shot pinged off metal. He fired again. *Ping!* And fired again.

Sven dropped.

What a shot!

But not done yet!

Ears ringing and knee screaming, Peter rolled onto his stomach. Swung his arms to aim the Glock at where Alicia—

She chopped the butt of her gun down on his hands. The Glock clattered uselessly to the dark-carpeted floor near her open door.

More than two feet away.

Peter tried to dive for it, even as his brain screamed in pain. But he got no leverage. He barely moved.

Alicia pounced, grabbed the Glock's grip with her left hand, and stepped back. She pointed her pistol at Peter's face.

It's over. Peter knew it. She was going to pull the trigger. No question. He'd rolled the dice and almost pulled it off. He'd at least killed that motherfucker Sven.

If only he could get hold of Alicia. He'd teach the fucking bitch a lesson or ten.

Alicia spun away from him, toward the back of the car. Pointing the gun at—

"*Lizzie!*"

Euphoria flooded through Peter. He wasn't dead yet after all! That fucking bitch Alicia had two guns and he had none, but she wasn't pointing either one of them at him now.

And why? Because Lizzie—*fucking Lizzie!*—was taking wide-eyed zombie steps toward Alicia and didn't seem to care that a gun was pointed at her! Just kept coming, her mouth moving as was Alicia's. Belatedly, Peter realized he couldn't hear either of them. Could only hear the deafening echo of the recent gunfire.

Jubilation erupted within him. He'd hit the long shot. Had had almost no chance at all, but could now pull the rabbit out of his hat.

Peter reached into his magician's sleeve on the underside of his right elbow for the pepper spray. Oh, baby, he'd done it! He'd done it! He could already see in his mind's eye that *fucking* bitch Alicia incapacitated, unable to see because of the pepper spray, and oh, baby, what he would do to the fucking bitch then.

He flicked the cap off the palm-sized spray bottle.

THE TRUNK HOOD POPPED UP. All above and around Lizzie, the night exploded.

Did you ever care for me at all? Lizzie had to know. *You tried to sell me as a twelve-year-old whore for pedophiles. Is that how you saw me? Did you ever care for me at all?*

A bullet whizzed by Lizzie's head.

Was it me, Peter?

Lizzie racked the slide. Extended her arm. Pulled the trigger. The huge man in the ski mask went down.

Am I that unlovable? Don't say it. I know the answer.

She climbed out of the trunk. Stepped toward the rear of the passenger side. Arm with the gun down at her side. A woman pointed a gun at her. Her back to the open front door, the woman said, "You're his woman! You're the woman he tried to sell!"

Was it me, Peter? It was, wasn't it?

Lizzie said it out loud. "Was it me, Peter? It was, wasn't it?"

She took another step. Two steps away from the woman. Almost at the open side door now. Looked at Peter.

"Was it me, Peter? Or was it you?"

A familiar gleam came to Peter's eyes. He reached into a sleeve at his elbow.

"Sell me to pedophiles?"

Peter pulled a small object out of his sleeve.

Lizzie extended her arm.

Aimed.

"Was it me, Peter? Or was it you?"

Peter pulled the cap off the small object. Reached his arm out to point it—

Lizzie pulled the trigger. Emptied the entire magazine. Dropped the gun.

"Peter, it was you."

TOO MANY IDIOTS, TOO FEW BOATS

INTRODUCTION TO TOO MANY IDIOTS, TOO FEW BOATS

Sometimes collisions can be a good thing.

As part of a workshop on writing larger than life characters (think Jack Reacher or James Bond), I needed to create one of my own, then write a story about him. At the same time, my great friend and thriller writer M.L. "Matt" Buchmann was starting a new magazine dedicated exclusively to thrillers. Other publications might include a few thrillers mixed in with other related genres, but *Thrill Ride – the Magazine* promised to be the first with a laser focus solely on that genre. The workshop assignment and Matt's announcement of the themes for the first four issues collided wonderfully.

Larger than life characters and thrillers make for the most perfect marriage, and I'd like to think "Too Many Idiots, Too Few Boats" is Exhibit A.

Matt bought the story with only the most minor of tweaks and featured it in the *Thrill Ride: Betrayal* issue. He then honored it with selection to *Best of Thrill Ride 2023*.

A most pleasant collision indeed.

TOO MANY IDIOTS, TOO FEW BOATS

Until the hurricane threatened to hit Key West like a Mike Tyson roundhouse hook to the temple, Jimmy Calderone was living the good life. Twenty-eight, single, his long blond locks flowing down to his shoulders, and without a care in the world. He worked as a featured street performer in Key West's world-renown Mallory Square, juggling everything from flaming torches to razor-sharp swords (at least they *appeared* razor sharp), all while riding on a ten-foot-high unicycle. He performed contortionist tricks, extricating himself from rings bound tightly around his arms and legs. And he did it all while cracking jokes that kept the audience laughing and more importantly, stuffing fives, tens, and even twenties in the black hat set up for tips.

He showed off his chiseled physique, deep brown tan, and washboard abs by performing bare-chested. It was part of his act. He'd flirt shamelessly and to great comic effect with obviously married women standing next to their husbands. And he got more than a few phone numbers or suggested places to rendezvous from single women stuffed in his tip hat or spoken aloud with seductive grins after the show.

Often, he followed through on the offers. As a lifelong resident of Key West, he considered it his civic duty to keep the female tourists satisfied and coming back for more.

Life was good. His mother had even stopped asking when he'd get a real job.

But if Hurricane Ernesto lived up to its billing, tonight's performances would be Jimmy's last for a very long time.

DEALING with hurricanes was a part of life in Florida. Ignoring hurricane warnings was also part of Florida life, at least for a gigantic majority of the population. There was always a new storm brewing, and TV meteorologists didn't manufacture spikes in their ratings by saying, "Don't worry about this one. It won't amount to anything."

So when meteorologists began talking about Hurricane Ernesto being a big one—and this time they really meant it—veterans of that nonsense rolled their eyes and let the gullible schmucks stock up on toilet paper and canned goods. Even when official evacuation orders came out, the vets kept rolling their eyes and living their lives.

Jimmy Calderone did plenty of eye-rolling himself, but it was at the idiots who'd put themselves in danger and then expect others to risk their lives rescuing them. One of those others was him.

He didn't advertise it because it was bad for his care-free image, bad for the show. But Mr. Not-A-Worry-in-the-World also had a very serious side as the lead volunteer member of the Key West Emergency Task Force.

"You need me to stick around and help pick up the pieces?" he'd asked Sherriff Nate Hawkins two days earlier, calling on his private cell phone number. Nate had been a close friend for almost a decade. African American, average height and build. Handsome, with a charming personality. "Or do I head for the hinterlands," Jimmy added, "and give you one fewer sorry butt to worry about?"

"I hate to put you in harm's way..." Nate said.

"But that's your job," Jimmy said. "And I live on Harm's Way Boulevard. Got it. I'll stick around. Call me if I can help."

Two days later, Jimmy called first. He had a logistics question but never got to ask it.

"I can't believe you just called," Nate said in a somber tone that made Jimmy think someone had died.

"What's wrong? The storm hasn't even hit landfall yet."

"Jimmy, this is spooky."

"Spooky? How?"

"There's a mission, but... it's hopeless. A suicide mission." Nate sighed. "The mayor suggested I send you, but I refused. I'm not going to sacrifice you. I just got off the phone with him. But then you called."

"What's the mission?"

"I can't."

"*What's the damned mission?*"

Nate drew in a deep breath through his nose. Jimmy could all but see his friend shaking his head.

"There's a fishing boat miles out to sea. The captain, his mate, and four tourists. *Buster's Revenge*, captained by Buster Johnson."

"I know Buster. Worked for him back in the day. Go ahead."

Jimmy had worked several fishing boats while still in high school and then continued until he perfected his street performer act enough to survive on the tips. He'd thought he might never get the smell of fish out of his nostrils and the salt off his skin.

Buster had pushed the envelope more than once going out in rough weather. If there was a buck to be made, especially a premium offered by a headstrong customer, he was game. And he always made it back.

But with a hurricane on the horizon?

"I don't know the details," Nate said, "but the boat is dead in the water. Probably a fried electrical system. Apparently, the tourists are a bunch of thrill seekers. Adrenaline junkies. The type that chase tornados and climb into shark cages. I'm guessing they offered Buster enough of a bonus that he couldn't turn them down. He thought he could dart out there and get back easily in time. Never expected Murphy's Law would kick him in the nuts with an electrical outage, or whatever the problem is, the one time he couldn't afford it."

"What about the Coast Guard?"

"They're swamped with other rescue efforts. Not

enough personnel and boats of their own. Or as my contact said, 'Too many idiots, too few boats.' They'll get to these clowns as soon as they can, but it'll be too late. We'll be at gale force winds soon and that means twenty-foot waves. Without power, that boat is going down. Even with power, Buster cut it too close. Those six idiots are going to a watery grave."

Jimmy swore softly but was confused. "What did the mayor suggest I do? Swim out there? I don't have a boat."

"At first, he wanted you to use one of ours in the Marine Unit," Nate said. "But ours aren't built for this kind of rescue. And even if they were, two are already in the shop and I'm using the rest to try to keep this city from blowing up. There are already multiple cases of looting boarded-up stores. The lunatics are coming out of the woodwork and I don't need to tell you that even on good days there are already more of them than sane people in this city."

"There's nothing you can do? Those six people are just going to die?"

"I can't let you make it seven," Nate said.

Again, Jimmy could all but see Nate shaking his head.

"How can I make it seven if there is no boat?" Jimmy said, barely holding himself back from exploding. "What am I missing?"

"You could steal the mayor's yacht."

Jimmy blinked and then blinked again. "*What?*"

"It's an appalling idea," Nate admitted. "Ethically bankrupt. It was bad enough that he was prepared to sacrifice you with one of our units. But this twist just makes it sick and perverted. That's why I refused to call you about it."

"*What?*" Jimmy asked again.

"If you succeed, then the mayor will say that he allowed you to commandeer the boat for the emergency rescue. You'll both be heroes, sharing the stage at the photo ops," Nate said. "But if you fail—and this is most certainly a suicide mission that not even you can pull off —then he'll betray you. Say you stole the boat, albeit with noble intentions, and we'll have seven watery graves and two sunk boats."

Jimmy took it all in. The mayor had always been effusive in his praise for Jimmy's volunteer work with the Emergency Task Force. Said the next drink was on him. Had seemed genuine. As if they were best buds. But it had all been glad-handing.

Now, Jimmy was nothing but chum for the shark of Hurricane Ernesto and the mayor's self-interest.

"Let me guess," Jimmy said, his eyes narrowed. "If I go down with the boat and it's considered stolen, the mayor cashes in on the insurance policy."

"You didn't hear it from me."

"Guess I'll have to disappoint the two-faced bastard."

NATE DROPPED him off shortly after noontime in an unmarked car two blocks from the marina. He'd spent the entire time begging Jimmy to reconsider, but it had been a waste of time.

Jimmy wasn't letting those people die.

Slamming the car door behind him, he sprinted the two blocks to the marina, then along the horizontal wooden planking that led to row after row of slips. Boat owners making belated preparations for the storm—loosening the bow lines, sealing off the windows, doors and hatches—looked up wide-eyed, their frayed nerves further startled by the pumping of his arms and legs, but then hurriedly returned to their tasks. Finally, Jimmy turned right onto the mayor's row and gasping, raced up to slip fifty-one.

He jumped directly onto the cockpit floor of the *Conch Paradise,* a luxurious Tiara Coupe 44. He shoved the key into the cabin door lock.

"Hey, what are you doing over there?" called out a reedy voice from the next slip.

A rail-thin, white-haired man wearing an aqua-colored Miami Dolphins baseball-style cap emerged from the cabin of the cruiser to Jimmy's left.

Jimmy figured that saying he was stealing the mayor's boat was not the right answer. Come to think of it, though, it would make a damned good addition to his act. The tourists would never believe it, of course, but his subconscious, which often dealt with stress this way, began putting the bit together.

He'd be juggling six flaming torches atop his ten-foot high unicycle and he'd begin the bit with, "This reminds me of the time I stole the mayor's boat."

He'd wait for what should be at least a smattering of laughs, then add, "Allegedly." Perhaps he could then ask audience members if they knew what the statute of limitations was on stealing a mayor's boat.

Of course, he had to survive what Nate had called a suicide mission to be able to ever use the bit. Not to mention restrain himself from strangling the six idiots—and even more satisfyingly, the mayor—and getting tossed in jail for life.

Piece of cake. Except perhaps for restraining himself and not strangling the idiots and the mayor. Especially the mayor.

It all flashed through his subconscious with lightning-fast speed while his conscious brain labored to come up with the best response he could manage, one both quick and designed to cut off any further discussion.

"Mayor's orders," Jimmy said, and ducked into the cabin. He tossed the starting key fob along with the cabin door key into the beverage well next to the steering wheel and pressed the start button. The twin Volvo diesels roared to life.

In a split second, he took in all the expensive furnishings, a built-in stove and convection oven, TV, stereo, refrigerator, polished teak table, leather chairs, and a couch. The smell of new leather, lemon cleanser, and salt filled the air. He could see a master bedroom below decks.

The forty-five-foot yacht was a magnificent tribute to craftsmanship, elegance, and opulence. Insanely more expensive than anything Jimmy had ever piloted. Even so, he couldn't help but feel slight disappointment.

It was built for luxury and comfort, not speed. Its cruising speed was thirty miles per hour and topped out at forty. Every extra minute spent getting to *Buster's*

Revenge amounted to a drop in the odds that he and the six idiots made it out of this storm alive.

On the other hand, Jimmy had to concede the Tiara Coupe 44 was sturdy as hell and sturdy was good. Sturdy was very, very good.

He dashed back out to untie the lines. Nate's unspoken message had been to be as inconspicuous as possible, if that even was possible, while getting the job done. Jimmy knew what he was doing. He'd been on boats since he was ten and had been licensed since the day he reached the legal age, but he also knew that even experienced boat hands sometimes panicked under pressure.

A major hurricane qualified as pressure. And racing off with the lines still tied, ripping the cleats to shreds, did not qualify as inconspicuous.

"Hey, aren't you that street performer?" the rail-thin, old guy said. "In Mallory Square?"

Jimmy loved his fans, at least the ones who left something in the tip hat, but this was not the time. His subconscious, mischievous as ever, suggested that he should explain that he was the brother of the mayor's mistress. Surely, the mayor's betrayal deserved at least that.

Mayor's mistress. Mayor's mistress. Definitely material for his act, but it needed a little something extra to finish off the punch. Perhaps that he was looking for a potentially embarrassing pair of panties left behind? On the right track. Panties were always on the right track. But not quite a comic bullseye. He'd need to work on it.

"Yeah, but gotta run," Jimmy said, unfurling one rope after another and tossing it aboard forcefully so it wouldn't snag. He grabbed a life jacket out of the storage unit up against the transom. As he slipped it over his head, he saw there were only three more. The idiots had better already be wearing theirs.

"You're pretty funny," the old man said with a chuckle.

I'm freaking hilarious, Jimmy corrected and darted into the cabin with a wave before the man could start recounting his favorite bits.

"Gotta run!" Jimmy yelled.

He pulled out of the slip, then made a hard left. He glanced down at the gas gauge and saw with relief that it registered almost full. That was a sight for sore eyes.

He reached the end of the slip row, seeing only one other man aboard his boat, racing out to look at him in astonishment.

Yes, Jimmy answered the unspoken question. *I am crazy.*

The no-wake zone extended a good deal further, but Jimmy ignored the restriction and pulled down the throttle. While you're stealing the mayor's boat, breaking the no-wake policy seemed akin to marine jaywalking. And when you're risking your life to save six idiots—on a mission spawned by the Benedict Arnold of a mayor—it seemed that all sins should be forgiven.

As he left the protection of the harbor, the salty wind howled outside. The whitecapped waves grew from choppy to increasingly high and rolling. Sitting in the captain's chair, enclosed in the sealed cabin, Jimmy kept the bow pointed into the waves. Soon, even a single large wave taken broadside would likely sink the boat.

Jimmy called on the radio.

"This is *Conch Paradise*. Calling for *Buster's Revenge*. Looking for an update on your position. Do you read me? Over."

No answer.

"This is *Conch Paradise*," he repeated. "Calling for *Buster's Revenge*. Looking for an update on your position. Do you read me? Over."

The *Paradise* rode up a wave and slapped down hard into a valley. Soon it was riding up a little higher on waves and slapping down a little harder, water spraying over the bow. The roller coaster action grew increasingly treacherous with seemingly every third or fourth wave.

Was his rescue attempt already in vain? Had *Buster's Revenge* already sunk?

"*This is* Conch Paradise," Jimmy yelled. "*Calling for* Buster's Revenge. *Looking for an update on your position. Do you read me? Over.*"

Nate had been right. This was a suicide mission. Suicide and pointless.

There was no way *Buster's Revenge* could still be afloat in this raging sea. There was no response because the boat had gone under, taking the six idiots—the six souls, Jimmy corrected into proper nautical language—down to their watery grave.

Rain pelted down noisily on the metal roof. The wipers furiously swung back and forth, clearing the windshield. A bitter taste filled Jimmy's mouth.

Six souls.

"This is *Conch Paradise*," Jimmy repeated yet again, wondering if it was time to call off this fool's errand and see if he could save himself. He couldn't give up, but at what point did he admit the obvious?

"This is *Buster's Revenge!* This is *Buster's Revenge!*" came the panicked reply. Static crackled through every word, but the message was clear. "*Help us! Hurry! Help us! Over!*"

Jimmy whooped for joy.

"Give me your updated position! Over!" Jimmy commanded. He was plenty damned capable of figuring out that they needed help. Don't state the obvious. Tell him what he didn't know.

The updated coordinates came in.

Jimmy swore and shook his head. "On my way! Over."

"You ain't the Coast Guard? Over."

"No, this is the *Conch Paradise*," Jimmy said. "Over." He wanted to add that the Coast Guard was too busy rescuing other brain-dead morons. Too many idiots, too few boats. But Jimmy bit his tongue.

"Ain't that the mayor's boat? Over." came the crackling, disbelieving question.

"I'm as close to the mayor as you're gonna get. Over."

"We're going to die!" screamed a voice in the background. "We're going to die!"

"Listen up! I haven't come this far to let you all die!" Jimmy yelled. "You are *not* going to die. I am on my way! Now get hold of yourselves and listen to me carefully." Jimmy waited a split second and then yelled, "A priest, a rabbi, and a fundamentalist walk into a bar..."

JIMMY'S HANDS clenched onto the boat's steering wheel so tightly his knuckles turned white. Sweat poured down his face, leaking off his forehead into his eyes, stinging them. He pulled close to the pitching and falling *Buster's Revenge*. The fishing boat's captain was performing a truly miraculous job of manually aligning the rudder without power to keep the bow pointed as much as possible in the right direction, into each wave, some of them fifteen feet high. Maybe even more. But after it slid down the crest of one wave, crashing into the valley, it was becoming perilously close to not making it up the next wave. In fact, sometimes it didn't but instead sliced barely *through* it.

Staying afloat by the slimmest of margins.

Soon, though, maybe on the very next wave, it would find itself skidding backwards down a wave that was simply just too high for it to handle, and the wave would crash over the boat, splintering it, and sending it down to the depths.

Jimmy tried desperately to align the *Conch Paradise* with the *Revenge* long enough and close enough for the other boat's mate to leap into the cockpit of the *Paradise* with a rope already tied to his boat, one he could use to lash the two boats together. Everything depended on that plan, communicated *en route* to Buster Johnson, captain of the *Revenge*. He'd been incredulous that Jimmy was alone and thus had no one who could assist in receiving a thrown rope, but eventually conceded that beggars couldn't be choosers and he was the beggar of all beggars.

According to the plan, while Jimmy tried to control the two boats lashed together, more than double the *Paradise*'s weight, the other members of the *Revenge* would leap onto the *Paradise*, the captain last of all, and then before the fishing boat's deadweight dragged them under, unlash it and set it free.

It would take a miracle.

But it all started with Jimmy bringing the *Paradise* safely alongside the pitching and bobbing *Revenge*, all while lining it up with the fifteen- to twenty-foot waves threatening to swallow up his own vessel.

Time after time, he came close. The life-jacketed mate, eyes wide with the knowledge of the odds stacked against them, was *almost* in position to make the leap. Then a wave tossed one of the two boats, usually the *Revenge*, off course just enough to make the attempt impossible.

Close, so close. But close wasn't good enough. This wasn't horseshoes or hand grenades.

Although it felt a lot like hand grenades with the pins already pulled.

Jimmy knew he had to do better. He had to be perfect.

He briefly wondered if this had been how the astronauts back in the day had felt when they'd had to dock two modules together in outer space.

Outer space, however, didn't feel like a productive thought. So another joining popped into his mind.

It's like sex, Jimmy told himself. *Relax and just let it happen.* His subconscious then added, *just find the right hole.*

Jimmy found the right hole.

The sides of the two boats touched, the scraping of metal on metal audible even over the roaring of the storm. The *Revenge*'s mate, rope wrapped once around his torso, sprang from the side of his boat and tumbled onto the Paradise's cockpit. Unfurling the rope, he sprang to his feet, staggered as a wave rolled, and lashed the rope to the *Paradise*'s nearest cleat.

A gap of about two feet remained between the two boats, now tethered imperfectly together. Alternately, they strained at the ties and then crashed sideways back together.

Jimmy strained to maintain *Paradise*'s position pointing into the waves even as the two boats crashed sideways together, veered two feet apart, and then crashed together again.

The deadweight of the larger fishing boat threatened to tear the steering wheel out of his fevered grasp. It felt like a giant, megaton anchor was lashed on the right.

"*Now!*" yelled the mate behind him. "*Now! Now! Now!*"

Jimmy felt the bounce in back of first one person, then another, and another. The cabin door opened. The storm's roar filled Jimmy's ears. One figure toppled in and then another.

The steering wheel tore at his hands.

He refused to let go.

Another person landed in back. Stumbled into the cabin.

How many? Jimmy had lost count.

"All aboard!" the Mate yelled. "Unlashing!"

And then it felt as though a giant anchor had been

cut loose off the right side. The *Paradise* rocked unsteadily side to side.

"All free!" yelled the Mate and dove into the cabin.

The *Paradise* plummeted down the highest wave so far—had to be twenty-feet high, maybe more—toward the trough below.

Was the angle too steep? Would they plunge nose-first into the depths?

Jimmy didn't know. It was close. Too close.

But they couldn't fail now. They couldn't plunge beneath the waves. Not after all of this.

The *Paradise* slammed into the base of the wave. Water surged over the bow. Bodies inside the cabin crashed against each other.

But the *Conch Paradise* bobbed back to the surface.

"*Yeah!*" Jimmy screamed fiercely like a warrior. "*Yeah! We're heading back! Yeah, baby!*

And when another Mount Everest-sized wave rocked the boat, and the unbidden thought popped into his mind that more deaths on Everest came on the way back down from the summit than on the ascent, he yelled, "*A priest, a rabbi, and a fundamentalist walk into a bar...*"

INSIDE THE HARBOR, Jimmy violated the no-wake zone with a righteous vengeance. *Fine me, sue me, jail me. Mr. Mayor, come after me with all you've got. No insurance money for you, you sonuvabitch!*

Jimmy's pent-up anger, suppressed for what had felt like forever so he could save the six idiots and his own sorry ass besides, exploded. If the mayor were here right now, the duplicitous bastard wouldn't have long to live.

Not yet, Jimmy told himself, trying to bottle back up his fury. *You're not done yet.*

Jimmy slowed the *Conch Paradise* only when the aisle between the two rows leading to the mayor's slip finally appeared. Jimmy let it chug to slip number fifty-one where, with the winds howling and rain cascading down from the heavens, he eased the boat into its slip.

Everyone on board whooped in unison. Tears flowed. Hugs were exchanged.

Jimmy shared their euphoria at having survived the impossible, but his was tempered with the knowledge that Hurricane Ernesto still hadn't even hit landfall. It would soon enough and who knew what damage it would wreak.

The worst was yet to come.

Jimmy suspected he'd have his hands full in the hours, days, and maybe even weeks to come. More than suspected. He *knew* he'd have his hands full.

He wondered what impossible task would be next. Whatever it was, it wouldn't be any more difficult than restraining himself the next time he saw the mayor, whenever that might be. That bastard had a nose that desperately needed to be punched.

A LONG SHOT WORTH BETTING ON

INTRODUCTION TO A LONG SHOT WORTH BETTING ON

You know a character has captured your attention when after the story's last line has been written, you still want more. Such is the case with Mick Flanagan, the protagonist in this story. He's an unconventional private eye who sets up shop in a seedy bar called Original Sin.

I was extremely proud of the story when it appeared in the inaugural issue of *Mystery, Crime, and Mayhem*. I became even more proud when the magazine's editor and publisher, Leah Cutter, selected the story (as she would do two years later for "Buried Braces") as one of her four editorial Derringer Award nominations.

Leah also arranged for a promotional event with actors associated with One House Productions reading selected opening scenes from that first issue. "A Long Shot Worth Betting On" was one of those privileged stories. The recordings of those scenes were then played during a Facebook Live event, after which a panel of the actors and writers discussed the production.

I fully realize that the odds of any of my stories or novels being made into a movie are microscopic. To be more specific, the required viewing device would need to be something like the TEAM 0.5 transmission electron microscope which took five years and cost twenty-seven million dollars to develop and can make images to a resolution half the width of a hydrogen atom. Yeah, it would take that slick puppy to provide a clear view of my chances.

(Although I do appreciate the many times fans have said, "You know, that would make a wonderful movie!" I agree wholeheartedly! Tell your movie mogul brother- or sister-in-law!)

All that said, the actor's reading of the story's opening scene grasped my heart and soul and would not let go. He got Mick Flanagan's voice just right. Nailed it. Creatively speaking, it was a narcotic experience that sent chills up and down my spine and through every artery, vein, and capillary in my body.

Yeah, I kinda, maybe, *would love* to see Mick Flanagan on the big screen.

Until then, you can follow up your reading of this story with *Pain Train*, the first in a series of Mick Flanagan novels. Depending on when you read this, *Pain Train* has either just released, has been out for a while (so look also for book two!), or if I've totally screwed the pooch, it's forthcoming any day now. (Sadly, the safest bet in all the world, every day, on any topic is that I've screwed the pooch.)

As for "A Long Shot Worth Betting On," it was also reprinted in *Pulphouse Fiction Magazine*. In the introduction, Dean Wesley Smith wrote, "I won't say anything about this story except that Dave can set a scene better than almost any writer working. Within a page I knew this place."

Settle in, then, and make yourself comfortable in the bar known as Original Sin.

A LONG SHOT WORTH BETTING ON

My eyes met Burnout's, two tables over at the back of Original Sin, the seediest bar in "Lynn, Lynn, City of Sin," and we nodded almost imperceptibly.

The bet was on. Forty-to-one odds with me the dog.

Pudgy and in his mid-twenties, Burnout was, as usual, stoned on weed, his eyes bloodshot and vacant, the pungent cloud that always surrounded him drifting over to me. Short with curly black hair, he's a one-man illicit pharmacy, doing a steady stream of business ranging from Oxy to blow to horse, reliant on the hard stuff now that weed is legal here in Massachusetts. He considers his stoner image a matter of advertising.

Other than us both wearing jeans and a faded T-shirt, I couldn't look any more different. My head is shaved. I'm six-two, two-hundred and thirty-five pounds, a dozen years removed from an All-Big-Ten career as a linebacker that hit anything that moved. Back then, fans bought jerseys with my number fifty-six on them and on Saturdays this time of year a hundred thousand of them packed into the stadium with perhaps millions more watching TV, cheering every time I knocked the living shit out of someone.

Now, my only applause when I crush one of the bad guys comes from satisfied customers. That, and the little demon inside me that needs to get fed every so often.

The subject of my wager with Burnout stood at the entrance to Original Sin, briefly letting some mid-afternoon light into the damp darkness before the door closed behind him. He visibly recoiled from the place, wincing. A big man, slightly larger than even myself with the look of a former body builder gone soft, he wore a tailored, dark blue suit and tie, and expensive-looking, impeccably shined shoes. A salesman, by my read, in his forties. A successful one, who perhaps had never been in a dump like this.

His eyes blinked rapidly, adjusting to the darkness as he scanned the half dozen drunks seated at the bar off to his right and the dozen square, wooden tables in front of him and to his left, arrayed in three rows of four. He touched his hand to a nose that had been broken a few times, perhaps wishing he could ward off the stale sweat of the drunks at the bar or the cloud of perfume from the table to his left where Tammy and Jasmine plied their mini-skirted, maxi-cleavage, blonde-wigged, soul-deadening trade.

My poetic side wondered if perhaps the guy recoiling was simply him shrinking away from Original Sin's pervasive shroud of despair and defeat. Yeah, sometimes I'm a real fucking Shakespeare. No autographs, please.

Turns out the guy wasn't a new patron of Tammy, Jasmine, or Burnout, the three favorites in the wager. He was here for the dog. Me.

"Mick Flanagan?" he asked as he approached my table in the dark, far diagonal corner from the entrance, eyes narrowed, wary.

I nodded and pointed to the chair opposite me, as two tables to my right Burnout shook his head and swore softly. He's never a good loser when paying off forty-to-one, but not smart enough to read the potential new clients to assess their likely reason for being here. Burnout is always willing to bet; I pick and choose based on my read. Of course, Burnout also plays the horses, showing on the left TV screen behind the bar, and Keno, its numbers flashing on the right TV. His business is all one gigantic gamble, one destined to destroy him sooner or later. Roll the dice until snake eyes carry you off to Hell.

Yup, more Shakespeare. Although perhaps I flatter myself and I'm just Dr. Phil, pretending Burnout's future is all that different from mine.

The source of my sudden forty-dollar bounty introduced himself as Gino Lombardi.

"Like Vince, the coach, but no relation," he said with a slight chuckle, shaking my hand and flashing a worn-out smile. I figured he used the line as an opener to so many sales pitches he said it on autopilot, not even thinking that a guy like me hardly needed reminding that a Hall of Famer like Vince Lombardi had been an NFL coach.

"What can I do for you?" I asked, as he took a seat.

Gino Lombardi leaned forward, huge shoulders hunched, his thick arms beneath the tailored suit resting on the dark wood, beer-stained table. Except for his suit, a stark contrast to my faded jeans and tight T-shirt, we probably looked like two heavyweight arm wrestlers about to do battle. At a classier bar, there'd have been a tablecloth and a colorful, laminated, propped-up menu in the middle of the four-chaired table, listing happy-hour specials and craft beers. At Original Sin, though, there is no tablecloth, no menu, no craft beers, and no hour that can remotely be called happy.

Lombardi glanced over at Burnout, twenty feet away with an empty table separating us. Burnout was staring vacantly straight ahead at the TVs, but got the message nonetheless. He headed for the door and, no doubt, a fatty.

Lombardi leaned halfway back in his chair, but still spoke in a whisper. "My son is in trouble."

I had guessed if it wasn't the vice that keeps me in business—a cheating spouse—it was a son or daughter problem, mostly likely a son. Boys get into more problems than girls, and fathers seem to head my way more often with the problems sons get into. I'm not instinctively viewed as a solution to girl problems other than busting the fucked-up head of an abusive boyfriend.

"What's your son done?" I asked.

Lombardi took a deep breath, squinted his eyes, and exhaled noisily through his nose. "I'm sure he hasn't actually done anything. It's all bullshit."

I waited.

Lombardi flushed. He swallowed hard, licked his lips, and looked off to the side.

I wondered if I was going to have to extract the entire situation from him one painful sentence at a time. If I could have pulled my phone out of my pants pocket and discreetly texted Burnout, I'd have asked for a wager on how long it would take Lombardi to spill the beans. Any line short of an hour, I'd have wanted the over.

"This is, um… kind of embarrassing," he said.

I wanted to ask, "Even worse than getting seen in this place?" but figured that might derail the guy even more. So I said nothing and waited.

Lombardi took a deep breath. "My son is getting blackmailed. Extorted, actually." He grimaced and shook his head. "By a skinny little runt prick my son could snap in two if he tried. It isn't even true what the little redheaded prick is saying, but…" Lombardi looked down at his hands. "… it still could ruin my boy."

Jimmy, the bartender, appeared at our table. Pushing fifty, he was tall and slender with a pockmarked face, gray hair tied back in a ponytail that hung halfway down his back. He wore a perpetually sour look on his face that made it appear he'd been sucking on lemons all day. He asked for Lombardi's order by wordlessly raising his right eyebrow.

Lombardi ordered a Jack-and-Coke. I said I'd have one as well, which Jimmy knew meant a Jack-and-Coke, hold the Jack. A guy like Burnout can sit in a place like Original Sin and get wasted, and for Tammy and Jasmine it's almost a job requirement, but I have to keep my wits about me. It's my business to read people at the same level a poker pro does to decide whether an opponent's play is a bluff or not. So I drink only enough to justify use of this table every day as my pathetic excuse for an office. And nothing stiffer than Coca-Cola.

"What's this kid saying about your boy?" I asked after Jimmy left.

"It isn't true," Lombardi said yet again.

I figured it either had to be something really, really awful—the worst of the felonies—or a specific something else. My money was on that specific something else.

Too bad Burnout wasn't taking action on that question, because Lombardi's next words confirmed my hunch. I'd have gotten paid off yet again.

"The little prick says my son is gay," Lombardi said in a hushed whisper. "Says he and my boy have... you know. Done shit with each other. Says he's got proof." He looked away and a flush came to his face. "It isn't true. Not my boy. It can't be."

I nodded. "I don't care if he's gay or not, but—"

"I do!" Lombardi said, stabbing himself in the chest with his index finger. "I fucking care! And it ain't true!"

I saw that one coming, too. Today, I'm fucking Nostradamus.

Jimmy brought our drinks. He'd barely set them down before Lombardi took one big gulp and then another.

"Tell me about your son," I said. "What's his name? How old is he? What's he like?"

"He's no queer, I'll tell you that." Lombardi stared down at the table's dark wood surface as if mesmerized by the three beer stains that Burnout contends forms a likeness of Abraham Lincoln. Of course, Burnout sees a lot of shit that ain't there. All I see are three dark mug-sized blobs, but there's no arguing the point.

"Tony—that's his name—is a junior at Lynn English," Lombardi said, his dark eyes brightening for the first time and a smile forming on the corners of his mouth. "Popular kid. Outgoing. Never a hint of trouble. Decent student. Not a genius, but good enough. Captain of the football team even though he's only a junior. He's getting recruited by all the best schools."

I knew this meant Alabama, Clemson, Ohio State, and the other major football schools, not Harvard, Yale, and MIT.

"He's a linebacker," Lombardi continued. "Almost as big as the two of us even though he's only sixteen. Hits like a fucking freight train. Just like you used to do. He'll be a star in college, just like you, but he won't wash out in the pros like you did." Lombardi winced. "No offense."

I waved it away.

"He's so much like you were," Lombardi said. "Only better. That's why I came here."

I gestured toward the drunks at the bar, then Tammy and Jasmine, their bare legs crossed, chewing gum. "You didn't come here for the ambience?"

Lombardi's eyes narrowed. "You think this is funny?"

I shrugged. "You shit on my pro career. I make a wisecrack."

"I heard that about you. A definite wiseass." Lombardi nodded. "Is that why you flopped in the NFL? Couldn't keep from mouthing off to the coaches? Always the smug smartass? Or were you just not good enough?" He glared at me. "Probably both. Well let me tell you, you couldn't hold my son's jock strap."

"But you're here because somebody has held it. And not a girl."

Lombardi shot to his feet, fists clenched and eyes bulging. His face was such a dark red, I thought it might explode. Through gritted teeth, he said, "It isn't true!"

My guess was that it was very much true, but I wasn't looking at the situation through the lens of a flaming homophobe like this kid's father. Lombardi couldn't accept that his superstar son was gay, no matter what the evidence.

I did understand part of his concern. There's no sport more homophobic than football, though sadly there might be many that are tied. Unless some fringe rookie became the first exception earlier this season and I missed it, not a single active NFL player has come out of the closet. And while Massachusetts might be a state with an accepting attitude toward gays, making same-sex marriage legal way back in 2004, and offering marriage licenses to back it up before any other state in the country, most of the college football powerhouses are in hostile territory.

Plus, even in supposedly liberal, open-minded Massachusetts, a lot of teenagers could be assholes, unbelievably cruel toward those who might be different than themselves.

So unless this kid, Tony Lombardi, was prepared to take the slingshots and arrows of a pioneer, he'd be facing some tough, probably ugly, challenges.

If it was true that he was gay. And maybe even if it wasn't.

"Sorry if I threw gasoline on the fire," I said. "You just got under my skin a little there. Let's settle down and figure this out."

Lombardi stared down at me for perhaps ten seconds before slowly sitting back down in his chair.

"He didn't do it!" Lombardi said, his voice shaking.

"Okay, tell me about the kid extorting your son."

Lombardi gulped the rest of his Jack-and-Coke, pounded the empty glass on the table, and whirled to look for Jimmy. Catching the bartender's eye, Lombardi raised his glass high, and Jimmy nodded.

"You good?" Lombardi asked, pointing to my still half-full glass of Jack-and-Coke, hold the Jack.

I nodded.

"Tell me when he's coming with my drink," Lombardi said. "I don't want to be talking with him sneaking up behind me."

"Gotcha."

Lombardi took a deep breath and began.

"The little prick's name is Lenny Shanahan." Lombardi gritted his teeth and squeezed his empty glass. "Thin as a rail, redheaded, and short. Girlish. No question he's gay. Fits every limp-wristed, swishy stereotype in the book. He fucking flaunts it! Can you believe that? As if he's *proud* of what he is! God, I hate the little prick."

"Bartender," I had to say, cursing Jimmy's timing now that Lombardi was actually opening up.

Lombardi blinked, then realized what I meant and fell silent. Jimmy put down Lombardi's drink, took the empty, and looked askance at my glass, his raised eyebrow a commentary on my failure to pay "sufficient rent" on my makeshift office. He walked away, shaking his head.

"I only met the little prick once," Lombardi said, after a big swallow of his drink. "I work pretty long hours. I'm in sales. I sell Toyotas on the Lynnway. Stop by and I'll give you a good deal. A big guy like you would look great in a new Tacoma. Lots of room. It's what my son drives. I'll give you a rock bottom price. Barely above cost."

I nodded idly at the advertisement-on-autopilot, and he resumed.

"But this one time I got home a little earlier than usual," Lombardi said. "This was after the little prick started giving Tony a hard time. He was up in Tony's room and they were arguing. You could hear them, although you couldn't make out the words. I asked my wife, Lisa, who it was and she just said it was Tony's friend.

"Eventually, the little queer comes downstairs, prancing about all swishy and everything. I kicked him out. Told him his kind wasn't welcome in our home. Tony and Lisa called me a homophobe—can you believe that? —so I asked them what the fuck they were thinking, having trash like that in our house.

"Next thing you know, I'm finding out from Tony that this Lenny kid is claiming the two of them had a relation-ship. *A relationship!* Can you fucking believe it? *With Tony!* And supposedly this kid has proof! Says Tony is the love of his life and he isn't going to let Tony leave." Lombardi looked like he wanted to puke. "Says they can be secret lovers—*secret fucking lovers!*—but if Tony leaves, the secret will be out. Everyone will know that Tony is as gay as he is!"

Lombardi gulped his drink. "It's a lie, of course! An outrageous lie! Extortion of the worst kind!"

Holy shit, I thought. This one could get ugly.

Could?

This one was definitely going to get ugly.

Then Lombardi took things to an even uglier level, or at least tried to.

"Tomorrow is Thursday," he said, leaning forward and dropping down to a whisper. "I'll be at work and so will Lisa, with plenty of witnesses. Tony will be at football practice. Three-thirty or four will be the perfect time to take care of this."

I blinked.

"How much do you charge?" Lombardi asked. "To clean up this mess. Evidence included, if there actually is any." He looked me dead in the eye. "Permanently."

Whoa! I knew my reputation was shady, but I didn't realize it was *that* dark.

"I'm a private eye," I said. "Not a hit man."

"Yeah, yeah," Lombardi said with a dismissive wave. He held his arms out wide. "I ain't wired. Check me."

"I'm not a hit man."

Lombardi took that in. "Is this, like, an Irish-Italian thing? I knew that could be a problem back in the day, but now?" He didn't get it. "Or because both of you are Micks? You a Flanagan and the little prick a Shanahan?"

"I'm not a hit man," I repeated. "I don't break the law."

Then, realizing what I'd just said, I quickly added, "Unless I have to."

"You work out of a place like this... and you're legit?"

I nodded. And didn't that just sum up my life perfectly?

Lombardi shook his head. "How are you going to take care of a problem like this without...?" He cocked his head, looking for an answer.

Good fucking question.

I PICKED Tony Lombardi up after football practice that afternoon in my battered, fifteen-year-old, four-door sedan. He compared my license plate with what his father had texted him, looked again as if in disbelief he'd be expected to ride in my rusty bucket of bolts, then hustled over, nervously checking to see if anyone was looking.

He was, as advertised, a good-looking kid, almost as big as me, with wary, untrusting eyes, a five-o'clock shadow, and thick, jet black hair, still wet from his post-practice shower. He wore a tan, thin jacket and matching slacks.

"No offense," he said as I took off, heading in the general direction of his house, "but what is this piece of shit you're driving?" His cloth seat cover was worn all the way through. A half dozen empty Coke cans and crumpled trash littered the floor at his feet where his expensive brown shoes looked totally out of place. A crack had begun to form in the windshield directly ahead of him. A musty smell filled the air. "And who the fuck are you?"

"Nice!" I said. "How 'bout them Patriots?"

He glared at me in much the same way his father had hours earlier. Genetics.

"Seriously," Tony said. "I've never met you before in my life, and next thing I know my father is texting me that I need to talk to you. *Or else.* What's this about?"

Great. The father hadn't even told the kid what this was about. Although I had to figure that beneath the bluster, he knew.

"I'm supposed to help you," I said, and watched for his reaction as much as I could while also keeping my eyes on the road.

His shoulders sagged, but he tried to maintain the bluff. "With what?"

"With figuring out how to tie your fucking shoes. What do you think?"

His whole body sagged. He closed his eyes and leaned his head back against the headrest.

"Lenny," he said.

"Yeah, Lenny."

Suddenly, the car was a whole lot more quiet.

"You want to tell me about it?" I asked.

"My father didn't tell you?"

"I need to hear it from you."

A look of total despair came over his face. He shook his head as if in disbelief at his plight.

"Before I say a thing," he said, "you have to promise not to hurt him."

And with those words, Tony canceled all his father's

protestations that Lenny's claims were just a lie. I could see it in Tony's eyes and hear it in his voice. He and Lenny had been a couple, and perhaps still were.

"I could promise not to touch him," I said. "But I'm not a very honest person."

Tony swore under his breath. He clenched his fists. His eyes shot bolts of fiery anger at me, then he looked away.

"Then fuck you. I ain't saying a thing."

"Listen, I'm no leg breaker," I said, thinking that I could make the wisecrack that I prefer breaking arms. Instead, I tried logic. "I'm not going to hold your lover out of a fifth-floor window. But if he's extorting you, I can't make a blanket statement that ties my hands behind my back. I need to protect you however I can."

I thought of adding, out of pure honesty, "even if it gets messy," but thought that might shut this kid up forever. Besides, honesty has never been my strong suit. Lies by omission qualify in my book as the God's honest truth.

Tony Lombardi stared sullenly ahead.

I noticed he hadn't corrected my reference to Lenny as "your lover." Perhaps he was intent on maintaining his silence no matter what. Or perhaps his subconscious hadn't noticed it because it was the truth.

Yup, I'm part Sigmund Freud, too. Or maybe Sherlock Holmes.

We'd been sitting at the stop light at Wyoma Square where the two lanes of Broadway fork into a single lane of Lynnfield Street on the left and Broadway continues on the right. A dozen or so one- and two-story brick buildings housing small businesses surrounded us, ranging from a package store to an insurance agent and realtor to a sports bar. Ahead, in the middle of the fork, was a 7-Eleven. When the light turned green, I took the left onto Lynnfield Street, then an immediate left onto the first side street and pulled to the curb.

"What are you doing? I don't live here!" Tony asked, alarmed, eyes wide, the pitch in his voice rising. He yanked at his door handle, but it was locked.

"Relax. We're here for a pizza." I pointed to my left. "Fauci's. I called ahead. You are hungry, aren't you?"

Tony nodded. "Starving."

I texted that we had arrived and within a minute, an attractive teenage girl, her brown hair tied back in a ponytail, brought us our large pizza. She smiled at Tony, but ignored me other than taking my money. I opened the box, held it out to Tony, and soon the smell of tomato sauce, cheese, and garlic filled the car.

"I was always starving after football practice, too." I said, and we both began to eat. Tony didn't just eat the slices, cut into Fauci's characteristic square pieces. He inhaled them.

"Thanks," he said after his third slice, his mouth still half full while he reached for another. "But if you think I'm going to flip on Lenny just because you bought me a pizza, you got another thing coming. I ain't bought that easy."

I considered saying that I didn't feel the need to buy what I could take by force, if necessary, but my considerable diplomatic skills kicked in and I remained quiet for another couple slices.

"Thing is," I finally said, breaking a silence that had only been interrupted by the sounds of chewing and groans of dietary satisfaction. "I may be more the type to buy you a pizza to get you on my good side than dangle Lenny out of a fifth-story window, but if you're not going to talk to me, I just might have to find a fifth-story window after all."

Tony froze in mid-bite of his half-eaten slice. His eyes locked on mine as he lowered the slice to his lap, then tossed it in the mostly empty box between us. He wiped his greasy fingers off on the napkins I'd put on the dashboard.

"Fuck you," he said.

"I'm going to help you whether you like it or not."

He glared at me.

"The more you tell me," I said, "the less I have to beat out of Lenny."

"Motherfucker!" he said, and ran his fingers through his now-dry hair. He shook his head, and closed his eyes.

The car got very quiet. I shrugged and grabbed another slice of pizza.

"Motherfucker!" he said again, perhaps thinking I hadn't heard him the first time.

Then he started talking. At first, he recited the same story his father had told me, replete with the same denials, except that where the father's telling was full of fury and venom, Tony's was hollow and half-hearted.

A wooden reading of a memorized script.

When he finished, I asked, "You expect me to believe that shit?"

"What do you mean?"

"Your father has convinced himself that it just might be true that you aren't gay because he can't handle the alternative. So he's buying the long shot even though he knows deep down there's only a sliver of a chance, if that. He's desperately going to cling to that lie until the ship goes down because he can't help himself.

"You, however, know better. You don't believe that bullshit. You can't. And you're a horseshit actor. So let's can the crap that nothing happened between you and Lenny, and figure out what to do next."

"Lenny could have convinced you."

"Convinced me of what? According to your father, Lenny is as openly gay as Nathan Lane in *The Birdcage*."

Tony smiled sadly. "I mean Lenny is a great actor. He could convince you of anything. He does come across a lot like Nathan Lane in that role, but Lenny can act straight as an arrow if he wants to. He's the star of the Drama Club. Always plays the lead male role." Tony snorted. "He could play the female lead, too, if they'd let him. He'll be a star on Broadway someday. Or in Hollywood. He'll be famous. Just wait and see."

I nodded. "You're pretty proud of a kid who's threatening to make your life a living hell."

Tony flushed.

"Listen, you know you're gay, and I know you're gay. Or you at least had a thing, and probably still do, for Lenny. And something physical happened between you two." I tried to lock eyes with Tony, but he just looked away. So I said, "I need you to tell me the exact truth so I can help you. I'm on your side. I don't care if you're gay, bi, confused, or trans. I don't give a shit. What I do give a shit about is doing my job, which is helping you. And my hands are tied behind my back if you're just going to feed me the same load of shit I heard from your father."

Tony bowed his head, closed his eyes, and shook his head. He breathed in deeply.

"Okay, I'll tell you everything," he said. "But I'll deny I ever said it."

"Fair enough. Get talking."

Tony studied his hands. He grabbed a slice of pizza and devoured it in scant seconds.

"So maybe I am gay." For what must have been the tenth time at least, he shook his head. "But I can't be out of the closet. Not like Lenny. Plenty of actors are gay. Hell, on Broadway it's almost a requirement."

Tony grinned weakly.

"Football is different," he continued. "It's as macho of a sport as there is. There's a reason no one in the NFL comes out, at least not while they're still playing. One of my teammates once said if he found out anyone on the team was gay—although he used the F word instead—he'd get his father's gun and shoot the guy's balls off. 'I ain't having some queer checking out my ass in the show-ers,' he said. And everyone else—there were about a dozen of us—nodded our heads and agreed." Tony closed his eyes. "Including me. I even added that after I shot the guy's balls off—and I used the F word, too—my next shot would be up the ass. 'Because that's where homos like it.'"

Tony breathed loudly through his nose.

"That's how it is with football, and that's how it's going to be until some superstar comes out," he said. "Not some high school kid that no one gives a shit about.

"I need football. It's my life. So I've got to stay in the closet. Deep in the closet. I've got to pretend for the college coaches recruiting me that I have a girlfriend. That I won't be a distraction. That I won't be the guy someone wants to get a gun for to shoot my balls off. Then give me another shot up the ass because 'that's where homos like it.'

"It ain't enough for me to be a star on the football field. I need to be straight, or be damned convincing about it, off the field." He stared straight ahead. "Or my future gets flushed down the toilet."

He turned to face me. I nodded. I got it. I knew the stakes.

"What happened between you and Lenny?" I asked softly.

Tony winced, and took another deep breath.

"We, um, were, you know…"

"Lovers."

"Yeah." Tony looked at his hands again. "For almost six months. And it was great. We had to keep it secret, but it was great. Until that guy talked about blowing his gay teammate's nuts off. And then I had to top what he'd said, because I was so damned terrified someone would suspect what I was. Terrified that maybe somebody *already* suspected what I was."

Tony grabbed the last slice of pizza and wolfed it down.

"The next day, I tried to break it off with Lenny," he continued. "He went ballistic. Especially when I explained why. He said that we—all gays, all members of the LGBTQ community—would never be free until cowards like me actually come out. Actually show pride in what we are.

"But if I couldn't out myself, he'd respect for now my need to stay in the closet—well, he wouldn't *respect* it... he *wants* me to come out and says it's my obligation... but he'd *accept* my decision and keep quiet about it—as long as we stayed together. But if I was going to leave him, he said, what did he have to lose? He was going to follow his conscience, not mine.

"And he'd out me. He said he had proof. Pictures. Of us in his bedroom."

Tony spread his hands wide, palms up. End of story.

"Do you think he does have pictures?" I asked. "Have you seen them?"

Tony shook his head. "No, I haven't seen them. I'm not sure they even exist. It's probably a bluff. But I'm not sure it even matters. He doesn't need photos to out me. He doesn't need photos to make nine out of every ten college coaches cross me off their lists, if not ninety-nine out of a hundred and every single one of them at the top schools. He talks and suddenly I'm not worth the trouble."

Tony took a deep breath, and he shook his head yet again.

"So we're back together, Lenny and me. Him, all the way out. Me, all the way in the back of the deepest closet. Huddled there in the dark, shivering, until he decides to open that closet door and expose me for what I really am." Tony looked me sadly in the eye. "It's a loaded gun pointed at my head."

FUMBLING IN THE DARKNESS, I pressed the doorbell at the Shanahan residence. Inside, a chime rang. A light went on beside the door, illuminating the small wooden porch I stood on to the left of a large picture window. The house, located on the right side of a quiet, dead-end side street in a blue collar neighborhood a half mile from Union Hospital—a place where I'd gotten a few stitches and sent other guys for a shit-ton more—was a modest split-level with a short paved driveway to the left and a one-car garage beneath an apparent windowed bedroom or study. A black SUV sat parked in the driveway, filling it to capacity, so I had parked on the street beneath a streetlight and beside a short, paved walkway to the porch. The house was packed in sardine-style between its neighbors, as was typical in this city, with a postage stamp-sized lawn and waist-high hedges marking the property boundaries on both sides.

The door opened two inches, then caught on the chain latch. A face peered out.

I asked for Lenny.

A second later, the door flung open. A balding man in his forties with a pronounced beer belly and dark-rimmed glasses glared at me, a dark hallway behind him. His nostrils flared. He clenched his fists and gritted his teeth.

"You piece of shit! I ought to beat the living crap out of you."

At first, I didn't get it. I spread my arms wide. "Take your best shot, motherfucker."

"Yeah," the man said, his face in a grimace. "He likes

'em big and tough. But you? You're old enough to be his father, you fucking pervert."

Light finally dawned.

"Oh! No! Not that!" I said, my eyes widening. I put my hand out in a stop sign. I was appalled at what he thought I was. And I don't appall easy. "That's not what I'm here for."

The man's jaw set. "Then what are you here for?"

That was a helluva question. I couldn't exactly say that I wanted a look in his son's bedroom. And not just any look, but one to see if his son might have taken photographs of him having sex with the star of the football team. Although the gay sex part didn't seem to be a secret anymore, there really wasn't any acceptable answer for this man to why I was here.

It was something I would have been better prepared for if I'd been thinking straight, if my conversation with Tony Lombardi hadn't left me so rattled. I had considered what I should say to Lenny, but not to his parents.

I identified myself and showed my PI license, something I'd hoped to avoid, figuring if the kid answered the door, I might seem less threatening that way. That was opposite my usual *modus operandi*. Scaring the shit out of people who were giving my clients a hard time was how I did business. I was so far out of my comfort zone now, up felt like down and down felt like up.

"I have a confidential matter involving a client of mine that I'd like to discuss with Lenny," I said. "It shouldn't take long."

The man stared at me a long time, then asked me to wait. He slammed the door in my face, then returned with a smart phone. He took several pictures of me and then my PI license.

There went my options of dangling Lenny out of a fifth-floor window.

"Wait here," the father said. "I'll get him." As he walked away, he held the phone aloft and wiggled it so I'd be sure to see.

Lenny opened the door. He was short, barely five-six, rail thin, and pale with fiery red hair and a light smattering of freckles. He wore tight jeans and a lavender shirt with a swirling pattern on the shoulders. He looked me up and down.

"Let me guess. Tony."

I nodded. "Is there someplace we can speak in private?"

He looked over his shoulder. "Not in here," he said. "But I ain't hopping in your car and letting you make me a Missing Persons statistic."

"I'm not going to hurt you."

"*I'm not going to hurt you*," Lenny parroted back in a mocking sing-song replete with a limp wrist, the other hand on his hip. A full Nathan Lane. "Yeah, right!" he said angrily, all vestiges of Nathan Lane gone. "I'm not stupid." Lenny gave me a look that made me think that's exactly what he thought I was.

I found myself wishing this kid were an outlaw biker, a gangster, or a neo-Nazi skinhead. Or at least a bully. Someone I could break into little, tiny bits and still feel good about myself. Playing nice wasn't in my wheelhouse. It was barely in my repertoire at all.

"So where can we talk privately where you'll feel safe?"

"That's your problem, not mine."

He had a point.

"Your father has already taken a photo of my Private Investigator's license and of me personally." I pulled my car keys out of my pocket and my driver's license from my wallet, leaving my phone undisturbed in the other pocket. I held out my keys and driver's license. "You can leave these with your parents. If I meant you harm, I'd be easily identified with no means to flee. We can stand beside my car in plain view underneath the streetlight." I pointed to the picture window to my right. "One of your parents can watch us the whole time."

"As if they care," Lenny said bitterly. "If you sliced my head off and cut me up into little pieces, you'd be doing them a favor."

Whoa. I opened my mouth to respond, but found no words.

Lenny took my keys and driver's license, spun and left, strutting in another pretty good approximation of Nathan Lane, then returned. He slipped into a stylish black leather jacket, and we walked silently through the barely broken darkness to my car.

Lenny hopped on the hood on the passenger's side, the side closest to the house's front picture window, and with one foot resting on the fender, crossed his legs. I slid gingerly onto the driver's side of the still-warm hood, hoping the aging metal wouldn't collapse under our combined weight, two-hundred and thirty-five pounds of me, and roughly half that for Lenny.

Noting a female peering out from the left side of the picture window, I said, "Your mother's watching us. She must care about you."

"She just wants to make sure I don't do you on the hood of your car," Lenny said grimly. He touched a palm to his cheek and shook his head, wide-eyed. "Whatever would the neighbors say!"

What the holy hell was I supposed to say to that? None of this shit was up my dark alley. Incapable of a response, I blundered ahead.

"Tony told me the story," I said. "The real story, not the bullshit version his father spouts."

I waited.

Nothing.

"Tony cares for you," I said. "First thing he said to me was not to hurt you."

"Just like my parents."

I frowned. "What do you mean?"

"None of them wants me dead. But none of them wants me to really live."

I blinked. It was a helluva line. I repeated it to myself, and wondered how long it had taken Lenny to refine the wording, and how many times, like any consummate actor, he'd practiced the line, timing the pauses and getting the intonation just right. But even a well-rehearsed line—and this one had been well-rehearsed— comes from somewhere, and this one seemed to have come from deep within. Little Lenny had rocked me as sure as a Mike Tyson right hook.

Not only did I not know how to reply, I wasn't sure there *was* a reply. I nodded pensively, stalling. I thought some more about the comment, then frowned.

"Maybe that's true of your parents," I finally said. "Maybe they do want you to be what you're not. Or at least pretend to be. But not Tony." Feeling more Dr. Phil than Private Eye, I said, "You're the person he fell in love with."

"And I'm the person he dumped," Lenny said bitterly. "I had to force him to come back to me."

"He was afraid. He freaked out. He would have come back to you if you'd given him time."

Lenny looked at me doubtfully. He frowned. "You think so?"

"I know so! I'd bet the ranch on it."

"Maybe you're right," Lenny said, nodding sadly. "But he won't let people know that we're together, a couple. He's ashamed of us. He's ashamed of me."

"He can't let people know that you're a couple, but he's actually very proud of you," I said.

"Yeah, right!" Lenny muttered, and rolled his eyes.

"Oh, I'm right about that, and right about how he would have come back to you," I said. "Listen, I read people. I do it for a living. Sometimes it keeps me alive. Sometimes it makes me money. But I'm good at it. Better than most poker professionals. This afternoon, I won a forty-to-one bet based on just reading somebody."

I didn't mention that the huge stakes I put up were for all of one dollar, or that the read was on Tony's father, who'd come to Original Sin with the intent of hiring me to kill Lenny.

Details, details.

"Tony is just about the easiest guy in the world to read," I said. "When he talks about what a great actor you are, and how you're going to be famous someday, he is *so* proud of you. It's in his words, but even more, it's written all over his face and in his eyes. And what's also written there is how much he cares about you. He might as well have scribbled it with a big, black Sharpie. Trust me, I know this shit."

Lenny fell silent for a very long time.

"Yeah," he finally said, "but Tony also loves football. And football hates us."

There was that. The verbal Iron Mike Tyson strikes again. But I had a counterpunch prepared for that one.

"Tony needs you *and* football," I said. Then I channeled Dr. Phil again. "With only one of the two, he'll be incomplete. You destroy his football career and there's no way you two can be happy together. Let him have both."

Lenny said nothing.

"You're holding what amounts to a gun to Tony's head," I said. "Extortion, if you want to get technical about it. 'Stay with me or I'll blow your cover.' Not much of a basis of a relationship there. What happens the first time you two have a really big fight? You out him, and prove it with pictures."

Derision formed at the corner of Lenny's mouth for an instant, clear in the gleam of the streetlight, and then was gone. In that brief instant, I knew that there were no incriminating photographs. None. Lenny might be a hell of an actor, but he'd let slip with that one reaction. I knew it as certainly as I knew my own name. I'd bet the ranch on it with Burnout back at Original Sin if Burnout had the capability to pay off such a wager. And of course, if I had a ranch.

But could I bet Tony Lombardi's football career on my read of Lenny's reaction? I would if I had to, but I didn't want to. I have this thing about writing out checks on other people's accounts.

And Lenny didn't really need to have photographs to ruin Tony if he wanted to. Based on what I'd seen, and reinforced by Tony's own story about his homophobic teammate, a mere accusation might be sufficient to do the trick.

"You seem like a nice kid," I said. "Other than this extortion thing, of course."

No reaction.

"I could threaten you or try to intimidate you," I said. "You threaten Tony. I threaten you. Tit for tat. But I won't.

"Tony seems to think you've got quite a career ahead of you as an actor," I continued. "Probably on Broadway." I shrugged. "So if I was going to threaten you—which I'm not gonna do—I could bring up that phrase they say to actors. Break a leg? You know?"

Lenny looked over at the house's picture window. No one was there.

"And I could point out," I said, "that it's a phrase I'm familiar with. *Personally* familiar with it. *Intimately* familiar with it."

Lenny tried to look calm, and he almost pulled it off in the limited light from the streetlight above. But he wasn't *that* good an actor. Not yet, at least. He swallowed hard. A bead of sweat formed on his forehead even though the evening temperature was dropping.

"I could tell you—no, I could *promise* you—that the day you finally get your big break on Broadway, your first speaking role or maybe even your first lead role and in a major production, no less, that would be the day, *entirely coincidentally*, that you do break a leg.

"What a pity that would be. You'd lose your big break because of..." I shrugged and smiled. "... a big break. Terrible timing! And you know, that's the kind of promise I could quite comfortably make and deliver on." I leaned a bit closer. "Because that's the kind of thing I do."

I eyed Lenny. "But I'm not gonna do that. I could, but I won't. You want to know why?"

Lenny said nothing.

"Because you're a tough guy," I said. "That's how I read you. I'm twice your size. Tony's twice your size. Hell, Tony's father is twice your size. But you've been taking shit from assholes for so long that you're tougher than all of us. Maybe even all of us put together.

"So if I did something to you, I'd dammed well better kill you, cause if I didn't, you'd come back sooner or later and ram it right back up my ass." I blinked. "So to speak."

"So I don't want to test your courage," I said. "I ain't gonna try to scare you at all. Because you're the toughest motherfucker out there. Ain't no one can push you around.

"Am I right? Did I get my read of you right? Are you the toughest motherfucker out there?"

The hint of a grin formed at the corners of Lenny's mouth. He shrugged. "Maybe you got it right," he said, nodding. "Yeah, I am the toughest motherfucker out there." He broke into a wide grin.

"Now before I tell you how you're going to be the beloved star in this drama," I said, "I want to confirm another read of mine." Lenny looked at me quizzically. I knew I'd hooked him with the words 'star in this drama.' I continued. "I don't really need confirmation. This one's a dead certainty. But just to dot the 'i' and cross the 't'."

Lenny said nothing.

"There are no incriminating photos," I said.

Even in the modest gleam of the streetlights I saw Lenny's checks give a slight flush of confirmation. Which was all I needed.

"You never needed them," I said. "Because until the sport moves out of the Stone Age, an accusation can be as lethal as a photograph."

Lenny started to make a half-hearted denial, but then shrugged. "You're right." He nodded. "I made that up."

I hadn't had a moment of doubt. Too bad Burnout hadn't been around to take my action.

"So what's this about me being the beloved star in this drama?" Lenny asked.

I grinned inwardly. Had him hook, line, and sinker.

Surreptitiously, I slid my left hand into my pants pocket—my body shielding what I was doing from Lenny —thumbed alive my phone, and tapped a few practiced buttons to send the pre-programmed text.

Without my eyes ever leaving Lenny's lightly freckled face, I began the mental countdown.

"The drama can be a classic adventure tale, filled with suspense, or a love story, or a combination of the two," I said. "How often does the star in a movie have to make a great sacrifice for a friend, or for the person he loves, or for the common good? Frodo in *Lord of the Rings. Saving Private Ryan. Casablanca.*"

"*Titanic*," Lenny said, nodding.

"Exactly! Lenny, you can be the star of your drama, heroic in your sacrifice, doing what is oh-so-hard, supporting your closeted lover even while you are so very much out, keeping the secret of the man you love until he can finally escape that closet," I said. "You can be—you *will* be—heroic all the way to that happy finale because no star betrays his lover. The star is bravely heroic to the end.

"In this drama, maybe the curtain doesn't fall until Tony's career in the NFL ends, ten or fifteen or twenty years from now. Then he doesn't have to be quiet any longer. You helped him make it, closeted the whole way, because that's what he had to do. But you made it together, even while you achieved your own dreams on Broadway or in Hollywood.

"Far more likely, some NFL stars break the ice for Tony, maybe in just another year or two. The dam doesn't just crack and leak a little. It shatters and the truth gushes out. The number of stars and ordinary Joes who come out of the closet make it no longer a big deal to be gay, even in football. Tony doesn't have to wait any longer. He's set free. You both are free.

"Or perhaps Tony is the pioneer. He decides to shatter the barriers himself. And dammit, he succeeds. He emerges from the closet as the football hero who makes it possible for others to set themselves free. And you're Tony's guiding light the whole way. The inspiration. The true hero.

"Whatever the case, no matter how many years the drama takes to play out, you're the star the whole way. The leading man. The most difficult role. You supply the courage. You provide the foundation for it all to happen.

"Why? How? Because you're the toughest mother-fucker out there, and you are the heroic star in your own drama."

Lenny took it all in, sharp eyes wide.

"That's my read," I said. "Am I right?"

For a few seconds, Lenny didn't move. Then he nodded gravely.

"I want to hear it," I said. "Let's hear you say it. 'I'm the toughest motherfucker...' "

Lenny grinned. "I'm the toughest motherfucker out there."

"And..."

He cocked his head.

I gestured with my right hand, prodding him along. "And the heroic star.."

He smiled broadly. "And the heroic star in my own drama."

"Now memorize your lines!" I said. "Don't make me have to coach you next time."

Behind us, a car accelerated up the side street, approaching us, its headlights poking through the darkness. Lenny glanced over his shoulder.

A white, mid-sized pickup truck, a Toyota Tacoma, pulled up alongside, and stopped. Tony Lombardi slid out from behind the steering wheel, and stepped down from the cab.

"Well if it isn't your co-star," I said to Lenny, then amended my words. "Supporting actor."

Lenny grinned. Tony looked warily at me. "So?"

I motioned him over, but before he was halfway there, Lenny jumped off the hood of my car. He didn't need any cue cards.

"I'm the toughest motherfucker out there," he proclaimed to Tony, spreading his arms wide. "And the heroic star in my own drama!"

SOMETIMES, you just have to trust your read. There's no guarantee, no nicely tied bow atop a neatly wrapped package. The bad guy doesn't end up in jail, or better yet, six feet under. The good guy isn't the clear victor, on top of the world without a worry to cloud his sunny day. Instead, you have to believe in an uneasy truce, one you've negotiated between uneven lovers.

Maybe my talk with Lenny was nothing more than a short-lived pep talk that would fizzle out in a few days, leaving behind only the implied threats that I pretended not to make. But I don't think so. For reasons I can only call "trusting my read," I believe in those two kids.

Back at Original Sin, I put down a bet on them with Burnout. Of course, I couldn't describe the wager as Lenny and Tony staying together, and Lenny not blowing Tony's cover until Tony was good and ready to blow it himself. Officially, the bet is that Tony will make it in the NFL for at least three seasons, an admittedly much, much tougher bar to clear. A pro football washout like me knows just how tough. But it was the only way I could discreetly make the wager.

I got good odds, but to be honest, not good enough. It's a long shot and almost certainly a sucker bet. Who's to say Burnout will even be alive then to pay it off, or me to collect? So that makes it even more of a long shot, and I'm even more of a sucker to take it.

But every once in a while, you don't bet with your head. You bet with your heart.

You trust your read.

Thank you for your interest in my books.

DHH

NEWSLETTER

Be the first to know!

If you love my writing, my newsletter is a great way to keep up with new releases, special promotions, and other content that's only available to my newsletter subscribers.

What are you waiting for?

Sign up at www.hendricksonwriter.com/newsletter-free-story/ today!

ALSO BY DAVID H. HENDRICKSON

Novels: Romance

Body Check

No Defense

Romantic Concerto for Strings and Brass

Novels: Young Adult/Sports/Historical

Cracking the Ice

Offside

Offensive Foul

Bottom of the Ninth

The Rabbit Labelle Trilogy (Omnibus)

Novels: Humor/Crime

Bubba Goes for Broke

Novels: Mystery/Suspense

Pain Train (forthcoming)

Collections

Shimmers and Laughs: Eight Wildly Hilarious Tales

Death in the Serengeti and Other Stories: Ten Tales of Crime

The Boy in the Boxers and Other Stories of Sweet Romance

Hell of a Band: Twelve Fantasy Stories

Fighting the Dying Light: Stories of Aging

Cape Cod Chips, Wiener Dogs, and Swiping Left: Stories of Sweet Romance

The Soulmate Junkie and Other Stories of Fantasy & Science Fiction

Crime From Another Time: Stories of Mystery and Suspense (forthcoming)

Crime Fantastique: Stories of Mystery and Suspense (forthcoming)

Crime, Up Close and Personal: Stories of Mystery and Suspense (forthcoming)

Nonfiction

How to Get Your Book Into Schools and Double Your Income With Volume Sales

Travis Roy: Quadriplegia and a Life of Purpose

Hendu's Story: From Dream to Reality

ACKNOWLEDGMENTS

To Leah Cutter, Kristine Kathryn Rusch, Matt Buchman, Michael Bracken, and Trey R. Barker, the editors who believed in these stories.

To Annie Reed, the editor and cover designer of this collection, whose expertise, advice, and friendship I can always rely on.

To my readers, whose enthusiasm helps keep me going.

To my family and friends, who support me during the valleys and celebrate with me on the mountaintops.

And above all, to Brenda, The Best Wife Ever™, for always being there and filling life's journey with such joy.

ABOUT THE AUTHOR

David H. Hendrickson's first novel, *Cracking the Ice*, was praised by *Booklist* as "a gripping account of a courageous young man rising above evil." He has since published seven additional novels, including *Offside*, which has been adopted for high school student required reading.

His short fiction has appeared in *Best American Mystery Stories 2018*, *Ellery Queen's Mystery Magazine*, *Heart's Kiss*, *Mystery, Crime, and Mayhem*, almost every issue of *Pulphouse Fiction Magazine*, and numerous anthologies, including over a half dozen issues of *Fiction River*. He is a multi-finalist for the Derringer Award, and his story "Death in the Serengeti" was honored with the 2018 Derringer Award for Best Long Story.

He has published ten short story collections: *Shimmers and Laughs: Eight Wildly Hilarious Tales*; *Death in the Serengeti and Other Stories: Ten Tales of Crime*; *The Boy in the Boxers and Other Stories of Sweet Romance*; *Hell of a Band: Twelve Fantasy Stories*; *Fighting the Dying Light: Stories of Aging*; *Cape Cod Chips, Wiener Dogs, and Swiping Left: Stories of Sweet Romance*; *The Soulmate Junkie and Other Stories of Fantasy & Science Fiction*; and *Crime from Another Time: Stories of Mystery and Suspense*, *Crime Fantastique: Stories of Mystery and Suspense*, and *Crime, Up Close and Personal: Stories of Mystery and Suspense*.

Hendrickson has published over fifteen hundred works of nonfiction, most notably his first book for writers, *How to Get Your Book into Schools and Double Your Income with Volume Sales*, and also *Travis Roy: Quadriplegia and a Life of Purpose*. He has been honored with the Joe Concannon Hockey East Media Award and the Murray Kramer Scarlet Quill Award.

Visit him online at www.hendricksonwriter.com.

www.ingramcontent.com/pod-product-compliance
Lightning Source LLC
Chambersburg PA
CBHW060717190726
48289CB00002B/721